OPERATOR 5:
CRIME'S REIGN OF TERROR

SECRET SERVICE OPERATOR #5 ™

AMERICA'S UNDERCOVER ACE

CRIME'S REIGN OF TERROR

By Curtis Steele

STEEGER BOOKS • 2020

PUBLISHING HISTORY

"Crime's Reign of Terror" originally appeared in the April, 1936 (Vol. 7, No. 1) issue of *Operator #5* magazine. Copyright © 2020 by Argosy Communications, Inc. All rights reserved.

CHAPTER 1
A TRAP FOR G-MEN!

THE HUGE, tri-motored passenger plane of the East Coast Air Lines was three hours out of Miami on its daily run to New York. It was carrying a light load of five passengers: two motion picture actors returning from a short vacation in the Southland, a dredging engineer who had been supervising the dredging of Biscayne Bay, a lady buyer for a Miami department store, and a boy of fifteen or sixteen, with a freckled face, a pug nose, and lively, inquisitive, eager eyes.

Somehow, as the plane hurtled northward into the gathering dusk, a strange tenseness seemed to grip the passengers and crew. The two moving picture actors kept throwing nervous, restless glances back toward the freight compartment, where several dozen boxes were piled in orderly rows.

Of the five passengers, the freckle-faced boy was perhaps the least nervous. The lady buyer and the two actors were beginning to feel air-sick. The boy and the engineer were all right.

Ahead, in the control cubby, the pilot and his assistant seemed none too confident themselves.

One of the actors turned in his seat, and said to the engineer, behind him, nervously:

"I think it's a damned shame that they should have to ship all that money in a passenger plane! Suppose we should be attacked? We'd all be killed!"

1

B

The engineer shrugged. He too, turned and cast a glance at the rows of boxes. "Eleven million dollars is a lot of money," he murmured. "But I don't think we'll be attacked, anyway. We have an escort."

The actor followed his pointing finger. High above them, and

2

to the west, a swift, trim little plane was flying a course parallel to theirs. They could see the twin machine-guns snouting out from between the propellers of its two motors.

The freckle-faced boy gazed up at the escorting plane with

admiration. It was the kind of ship he would have liked to be flying himself.

The lady buyer, a young woman of twenty-eight or twenty-nine, was sitting directly behind the boy. He turned, found her looking at him, and smiled shyly. She smiled too, and said:

"You're quite young to be flying." Her face was a little pale with airsickness, but she was making a brave effort to control it "Is this your first trip?"

"No, ma'm. I've been up before."

The young woman leaned forward, forgetting her nausea a bit. She was interested in this quiet youngster who spoke so modestly with the air of a veteran traveler. "What is your name, young man?"

"Tim Donovan, ma'am." The boy turned in his seat, smiled at her. He refrained from telling her that he had flown planes himself, that in spite of his youth, he had in his pocket a special pilot's license issued by the United States Department of Commerce.

The actor who had addressed the engineer, was still worried about hold-ups. He interrupted, speaking loudly, so that everybody in the compartment had to listen to him. "I still think it's a damned shame that they should send all that money. Suppose the Scarlet Baron decides to attack us? He's pulled off some nasty jobs in the last few weeks. Even if that escort of ours fights him off, a stray bullet might send us down—"

THE RADIO operator, occupying the first seat, close to the control room, turned, frowning. "You won't have to worry about that money after we leave Savannah, sir," he said. "We're transferring it to a steamer there. We should be in Savannah in another half—"

He stopped, his eyes wide as he gazed, horror-struck, up through the window at their trim escort, flying above them. The others followed his gaze, and a hush of terror fell on the occupants of the compartment.

For three black, winged shapes had swooped down upon their guardian plane. They were Mack monoplanes, with machine-guns mounted on both wings. Upon the fuselage of each black hawk appeared a single letter "B", which shone brightly in the reflection of the riding lights.

Flame belched from six black snouts. Tracer bullets lanced into the escorting plane above them, and suddenly the little ship burst into fire, went spiraling toward the earth. It fluttered past the windows of the passenger plane, and the people in the compartment looked out, frozen with dread, at the flaming mass which had, just a few seconds before, been a trim, fighting unit. For one second they saw the aviator's face, framed in fire. Then the burning plane dropped past them like a plummet.

The freckle-faced boy bad watched the tragedy with clenched fists, bleak eyes. Now he saw the three black monoplanes swing in their course, and come flying alongside them. A helmeted figure leaned out of the cockpit of the leading plane, and motioned for them to land.

Within the compartment, panic reigned. The two actors had raised their voices in frightened shouts. The lady buyer was shrieking hysterically. Only the boy, Tim Donovan, and the dredging engineer preserved their poise.

The radio operator was shouting frantically into his radio. The pilot was clinging grimly to his wheel, driving the plane onward, while the co-pilot was bending over, breaking out weapons from a chest. It was evident that the crew did not intend to obey the raiders' commands.

The men in the black monoplane sensed this. Their leader raised his hand in a signal to the others. The three planes rose sharply, banked, and came driving back from above. Lead belched from their machine-guns, smashed the glass of the passenger compartment. The radio operator gasped, toppled from his seat with a ribbon of red sewn across his back where steel-jacketed slugs had caught him.

The other passengers jumped from their seats, choked the aisle. The pilot and his assistant turned white faces backward, then looked up at the three black planes rising again for another attack. The pilot groaned:

"We're licked! We've got to land!"

The boy, Tim Donovan, had seen the radio operator die. Now, he scrambled out of his seat, pushing the others aside unceremoniously, and stepped over the operator's body. He seated himself in the dead man's chair and reached frantically for the instrument board, adjusting the headphones to his ears.

His fingers moved swiftly, efficiently. Above the sounds of frantic passengers and the roar of the motors which hammered at them now through the broken windows, the boy's voice rose as he got his connection:

"MW-MW!" he was calling. "MW! Tim Donovan talking, aboard the East Coast Airliner! Communicate with H-7! We are being attacked over Georgia by three monoplanes of the Scarlet Baron! Being forced to land! Send out relief planes at once! We—"

Suddenly the breath was jarred out of him as the big plane bounced to an uneven landing. He was thrown violently from the chair, but scrambled to his feet and looked out. Luckily, there had been a field at this spot.

BRAKES SQUEALED as the pilot brought the plane to a halt. Two of the attackers slid to a landing close by, and four men, armed with sub-machine guns swarmed out of them. The third plane hovered above, circling around them, and acting as a lookout.

Slowly, the propellers of the airliner ceased their revolutions. The drone of the motors died, and the voice of the helmeted leader of the attacker was heard. "Come out of there, with your hands in the air!"

The pilot and co-pilot, their faces blanched, stepped from the control room with their hands raised. The pilot called to the passengers: "Better do what those fellows say. All they want is the money. They'll let as go after they get it!"

It was evident that he didn't believe his own words. But there was nothing else to do. The passengers filed out after the crew— all but Tim Donovan, who had climbed back into the seat, and was talking frantically once more into the radio phone.

Passengers and crew lined up outside, and the leader of the raiders, looking into the lighted compartment, saw the boy at the instrument. He snarled: "You! Kid! Come outta there!"

The boy didn't hear him, because of the earphones clamped to his ears. But he was looking at the man, saw his lips move, and knew what he was saying. Instead of obeying, he went on talking into the phone.

The helmeted man took a step forward, raised his sub-machine gun. A stream of lead spurted from it. But Tim Donovan had foreseen his movement, and had acted a split-second faster. He threw himself sideways from the chair to the floor of the compartment, and the hail of slugs tore into the wall above him. He fell on the bloody body of the dead radio operator, and lay still.

The man who had fired, grinned thinly. He thought he had killed the boy. "Wise kid, huh!" he snarled.

He stepped past the captive passengers and crew, motioned to his other men. Two of them followed him, while one remained to guard the prisoners. Inside the compartment, the leader cast only a single glance at the boy, lying in a pool of blood beside the dead man. He turned away, directed the others in the job of transferring the boxes of currency.

It took ten trips of the two men, while the leader watched. In fifteen minutes, the money was all in the two black planes.

Tim Donovan had lain quietly all this time, not daring to move....

Finally, the leader stepped out. His men had returned to their planes, which waited with racing motors. The leader backed away from the prisoners. His features were pinched, sharp, merciless. He called out to them:

"Thanks for the dough. You should've given up right away instead of trying to escape. Here's a little souvenir from the Scarlet Baron!"

As he finished speaking, he coolly raised his Thompson and sent a spray of whistling lead into the bodies of the passengers and crew. He kept his finger on the trip until the drum was empty and every one of them, including the pretty lady buyer, lay bloody and lifeless on the ground. Then, smiling, he stepped into his ship, and the two black pirate planes rose to join their lookout, disappeared into the night....

No one was left alive below, except for one small figure that scrambled out of the passenger compartment and stood shaking a fist up at the vanishing murderers.

Ten minutes later, two army planes sighted the flares that the boy had lighted. They were too late. The trail of the Scarlet Baron's murderous crew was cold....

IN NEW YORK CITY, in an office whose telephone number was listed in no directory, a black-haired man sat at a desk, frowning, while his stubby fingers drummed a nervous tattoo upon the glass top. The office door bore the apparently commonplace name of a commercial firm. In reality, this was the main New York office of the United States Secret Service. The man at the desk was the chief of the Intelligence, its active, directing head. He was known to his subordinates only as Z-7.

The cause of his displeasure, as evidenced by his frown, and the nervous drumming of his fingers, was a telegraph message on the desk before him. It was addressed to MW-NY—the official designation of this office—and had been routed through CG, the Chicago sub-head-quarters.

Z-7 thumped the desk, looked up at the gray-eyed, stocky man who sat opposite him. "I can't get this thing, Murdoch," he growled. "It's a message from Operator 5, my best man. But it's in a code I can't decipher! Can you beat that?"

Murdoch shrugged. "Let's put that aside, Z-7. We've got other things to worry about. Now this business down in Georgia. Where is this boy, Tim Donovan?"

"He's on his way here in one of the army planes that picked him up." Z-7 glanced at his watch. "He should be here in a few minutes."

He arose, paced up and down in the small office. "Look here, Murdoch. As Divisional Chief of the Federal Bureau of Investigation for the New York District you've got charge of all the G-Men in the territory. You've got charge of the campaign against the Scarlet Baron. All right, I won't butt in. But why don't you let me help you? I've got plenty of men—"

Murdoch raised a hand. "Sorry, Z-7, but I guess I can handle this business alone. I don't need the Intelligence. I grant you that the Scarlet Baron is a super-criminal, but we've handled tough eggs before. I'm working on a little plan that I expect will bag him tonight sure!"

Z-7 raised his eyebrows. "I hope to God you're right, Murdoch!"

The chief of the G-Men nodded complacently. "One of my best men, Alton Wiggins, has wormed himself into the Scarlet Baron's organization. He's going to give us the tip-off tonight, and we'll round up—"

He stopped as a knock sounded on the door. Z-7 barked impatiently: "Come in!"

The door opened, and Tim Donovan entered. His face was pale; his eyes reflected the tragedy he had witnessed down in Georgia a short time before.

Z-7 went to him quickly, put an arm about the lad's shoulders affectionately. "Glad to see you, Tim," he said warmly. "I want to present you to Ron Murdoch, Chief of the New York F.B.I. He's come here to hear your story. Naturally, the F.B.I. has charge of this business."

Tim shook hands with Murdoch, and Z-7 added in explanation:

"You see, Murdoch, Tim is a little too young to be officially appointed an Intelligence Agent. But he's been working as Operator 5's unofficial assistant. Too bad Operator 5 isn't here."

He stopped as he saw the impatience on Murdoch's face, and said hastily: "All right, Tim, go ahead and tell your story."

Swiftly and concisely, Tim related all that had happened. When he was through, Murdoch shook his head. "It's bad, bad! But we'll settle all this tonight. After tonight, we'll have a definite lead on the Scarlet Baron!"

CRIME'S REIGN OF TERROR

In an instant, the street was

turned into a shambles!

Tim looked doubtful. "I don't know, sir. He seems to be a pretty cagey bird. Of course, I'm only a kid—"

Murdoch smiled. "That's right, boy. Don't forget, the F.B.I. has put away some pretty tough babies. Why, even Barney Broon got his. He was public enemy number one, but now he's public convict number something-or-other—and he's down in Leander Prison for life. If we got Broon, we'll get this bloody Scarlet Baron, too!"

He shook hands with Z-7, and left.

Z-7 waited till he had gone, then turned to Tim Donovan. "Look here, Tim, I've got a message from Operator 5. But it's in an unregistered code. I thought you might know something about it."

He extended the sheet to the lad, who glanced at it and nodded. "That's the 'F' code. Jimmy worked it out so's he and I could have a private means of communicating with each other. I guess he figured you'd call me."

He took the sheet, pulled up a chair opposite Z-7, and sat down, with a pencil. In ten minutes, be had written a transcription of the message. His eyes were wide with eagerness as he handed it across to Z-7. "Gee, Chief, it looks like Jimmy is on a hot trail!"

The message read:

Am using this code because I fear a leak in the Intelligence Service. I will arrive in New York from Chicago on the twenty-seventh. Have Tim Donovan posted in front of Walnut Grove night-club between ten and ten-thirty tonight. Have him go down to headquarters, look at rogues' gallery pictures of men wanted by F.B.I. and observe if any enter during that time. I will arrive at ten-thirty. He will contact me in accordance with plan eleven. Necessary to maintain utmost secrecy. Tim must go alone. Believe I am on trail of Scarlet Baron.

—Operator 5

Z-7 raised his eyes from the boy's writing, and the glance of the two met for an instant.

"So Jimmy's on the trail of the Scarlet Baron!" Z-7 breathed. "It's not our province. The Department of Justice is handling it, and we have no right to interfere. You heard what Murdoch said."

"But look. Chief," Tim Donovan broke in. "Jimmy wouldn't be bothering with this thing if he didn't have something hot. Maybe he's just dug something up. I think he had that in mind when he said he wouldn't come to Florida with me for a rest. He's been in Chicago for six months now—"

"A strange way for him to spend his leave. When he asked for six months off, I thought he wanted to get married or something. Instead, he disappears—"

"You'll let me go, won't you, Chief?" Tim urged.

"I suppose so," Z-7 growled. "But when you see him, you tell him that he better not mix up in the Scarlet Baron business If the Department of Justice should complain about us to Washington, we'd have a job on our hands to explain why we don't stick to out own knitting!"

Tim Donovan was on his way out. "I'll tell him, Chief—if I remember!"

The door closed behind the boy, with a bang. And Z-7 smiled in spite of himself at the lad's exuberance....

IN NEW YORK'S Greenwich Village where Seventh Avenue meets Fourteenth Street, there is a large square into which a number of narrow streets converge.

In one of those streets is the two-story building which houses Mazzoli's Restaurant. Above the restaurant is a floor of private rooms. At one time, these private rooms had been rented to various organizations for meetings; but of late they seemed to have been occupied entirely by one outfit, whose name was lettered on each window as follows:

INTERNATIONAL SOCIAL CLUB

A separate doorway alongside the entrance to Mazzoli's led up to the meeting rooms by means of a narrow, rickety stairway. Though many men were often seen to enter through this narrow doorway, none knew where they came from. The residents of the neighborhood seemed strangely unwilling to talk about them or about the club. It was doubtful at best if they knew anything—for the International Social Club kept its business strictly private.

However, it appeared that a number of people were interested in the organization. For on this particular evening in February, while the slush of a wet snow lay like a dirty blanket on the streets, a man sat at the window of a room in the tenement house directly opposite. The room was in total darkness, and the window was open two or three inches at the bottom. Through this opening, the man was peering through a pair of night glasses at the windows of the International Social Club. Near him sat another man, with his hand on a Very pistol, ready to fire it out the window at a moment's notice. Both men were young, clean-cut. Their attitude was tense, expectant. They said not a word to each other. On the floor beside them lay two quick-firing rifles of the latest design, just adopted as regulation arms by the United States Department of Justice.

Outside, there were other men who were also inconspicuously interested in the rooms above Mazzoli's. At intervals during the last hour, several sedans had converged upon that street, from each of which three or four other clean-cut young men had emerged to scatter in the neighborhood.

The last of these cars to arrive pulled up at the curb about a hundred feet past Mazzoli's. Within it were three of the young men, and an older man who seemed to be in charge. The older man was Ron Murdoch, the Divisional Chief of the Federal Bureau of Investigation of the Department of Justice. The young men who were closing in on the meeting rooms of the International Social Club were his operatives—all college men who had chosen voluntarily the moderately paid, highly dangerous work of G-Men as their life careers.

Ron Murdoch's gray eyes scanned the dark corners of the street, and he nodded tensely as he noted the shadows in darkened entryways, noted the apparently casual figures strolling up and down.

He said to the driver of the car: "You can shut off the motor, Paulson. We'll stay here. They're all gathered upstairs by this time. There's no danger of their spotting us."

Paulson clicked off the ignition, turned a worried face to his chief. "Do you think Wiggins will be able to give us the tip-off, sir? If those birds should suspect him of being a Fed, instead of one of—"

"Why should they?" Murdoch demanded. "Wiggins has worked with them now for two months. I deliberately had him go slow. It's stuck in my crop to see them pull off the last couple of jobs. But I made him stick it out. Tonight, they've called a meeting of the whole crowd. It's our chance to nab them all at once—maybe the Scarlet Baron himself."

He glanced upward at the third floor window of the tenement. "Everything is planned down to a 'T'. At the right time, Wiggins will say it's stuffy in there, and open the window. When he opens it, Crocker up there, lets off the Very pistol. And we take them."

At that moment, a Black-and-Tan cab pulled up right in front of Mazzoli's restaurant, and a young man got out of it, apparently drunk. He started to argue good-naturedly with the cabman about the amount of the fare.

Murdoch, still looking through the rear window of the sedan, chuckled. "And that's how Wiggins makes his escape from the club rooms, Paulson. That's our cab. Its top is made of special elastic material. All Wiggins has to do is jump from the window, and land on it. I hope those boys can manage to keep up their argument till this thing breaks. Once Wiggins is out, we'll blast them from front and back!" He motioned to one of the young men who sat beside him. "Break out the gas bombs. Get them ready."

All was silent along the dark street, except for the good-natured argument of the cab-driver and his inebriated fare....

BACK AT the corner of Seventh Avenue, a huge, long-distance moving-van tried to swing into the narrow street, and got stuck at the turn. The driver swore luridly from the glass-enclosed compartment of his cab, tried to back her out again.

Murdoch's eyes narrowed as he watched the truck driver's efforts, and he muttered: "I wish that damn fool would get out of here. He's making such a racket with his back-fire. Larry—" he addressed another of the young men in the rear seat with him—"go out there and tell that chap not to enter this street. Get him out of here!"

The young man addressed as Larry said: "Right, sir," and started to open the door. But Paulson, behind the wheel, stopped him.

"Just a moment, sir. Maybe the van is a good thing right there. If any of those birds from the International Club should try to make a break for it in a car, that van would block them!"

Murdoch nodded. "You're right, Paulson. Never mind, Larry." He chewed his under lip. "Though when we get going on those babies, they won't be in any condition to make any breaks! They—"

He broke off. For at that moment, one of the glazed windows of the International Club was raised. In the light that streamed from the room behind that window there was outlined, for an instant, the figure of a slim man.

Murdoch exclaimed: "That's Wiggins!"

Things began to happen.

19

From the third-floor window of the tenement opposite, a Very pistol flamed, and the flare rose high above the roof of the building so that it was visible to the men posted behind Mazzoli's restaurant as well as to those in the street in front.

The figure of Wiggins climbed the sill of the International Club window, leaped to the roof of the taxicab below, while guns roared and flame belched at him from the room he had left. But he had moved fast, and he landed on the cab, bounced off on his feet on the sidewalk beside the cabby and the passenger. Simultaneously, shadowy figures darted out from entryways and hallways, debouching into the street, carrying high-powered quick-firing rifles and submachine guns. Other figures ran from parked cars, holding grenades and gas bombs ready to throw. The street was abruptly filled with G-Men. Flame lanced up from two dozen weapons at the windows of the International Club. The attack was launched!

Murdoch and his men piled out of the sedan, and the grizzled chief took command of the attacking party. Wiggins ran over to him, gasped breathlessly:

"It's all set, Chief. They haven't got more than two rounds of ammunition. They had the machine-gun clips stocked in the bath-tub. I came up early tonight, and turned the water on. Their ammunition is all soaking wet, and no good. As soon as they exhaust what they have in their small arms, you can toss in a couple of gas bombs and take 'em all alive!"

Murdoch nodded. "Good man!" Then he raised his voice in command. "Spread out, boys, and hold your fire. Prepare gas bombs!"

IT WAS then that the stalled van at the corner swung into action. Loopholes appeared in its sides as if by magic. And from those sly loopholes, a withering machine-gun fire was poured into the government men in the street. A hail of lead swept through them in a murderous blast which cut them down mercilessly. Taken unawares, they had not even time to reach cover. In an instant the gutter was turned into a shambles. Dying men writhed on the ground. Others, mortally wounded, raised their weapons with a last effort, and fired at the truck. Their slugs bounced off the side of that van like so many rubber balls. It was made completely of steel—bullet-proof....

Murdoch, with blood spurting from his chest and nose and mouth, raised himself on one elbow. Dying, he managed to lift his service revolver, fired with grim precision. "God forgive me," he said. "I've led them into—a trap!" And he fell, lifeless, into the slush.

Of the close to fifty F.B.I. men who had been in that street, none were left on their feet, except for a scant half dozen who had sought the sanctuary of doorways at either side. Now the staccato death-march of machine-gun lead sought them out too, piercing the flimsy wood-and-glass shelter of the store fronts where they crouched, fighting to the last.

Soon there were none left to fight. The street was littered with dead. There were no wounded, for the raking fire from the truck had combed the gutter again and again, hurling hot lead into already wounded men, making sure that there was no spark of life left in them.

And only then did the firing cease.

At once, the doorway of the International Club opened, and dark figures ran out swiftly, piled into a side door of the van, which had been thrown open. The door closed, and the van backed out of the street, roared away up Seventh Avenue with throttle wide open, disappeared into the night.

Police whistles shrilled, sirens screamed, as squad cars raced to the scene. Shattered glass, dead bodies and oozing blood littered the street in front of Mazzoli's restaurant. Only one man, white-faced, with death's-head eyes, remained alive in that shambles. It was Paulson, the driver of Ron Murdoch's sedan. Shaking as if with the plague, he stepped from the car. He had not come out with the others when the attack began, but had crouched at the bottom of the car, had fired his revolver into the air.

Now, however, he emerged. His eyes swept the litter of mangled bodies of his brother officers. He stooped quickly, stretched himself at full length in the slushy gutter, rubbed his coat and face into the bloody wounds of one of the dead men.

Then, just as the first of the police appeared around the corner, he tottered to his feet, a bloody, disheveled figure—the only survivor of the merciless massacre. There was on his face the same expression which Judas Iscariot must have worn when he went to collect his thirty pieces of silver....

SEVENTH AVENUE is a long thoroughfare. It extends north and south through the heart of Manhattan, and it runs the gamut of every type of neighborhood with which New York is blessed—or cursed. At its southern extremity is Greenwich Village; at its northern end is Harlem, the heart of the Black Belt, where disease breeds, where lotteries take the last dimes of men, women and children; where knives flash in the dark, and policemen patrol in pairs. Here, too, are numerous night clubs, "hot spots" of the city, where men and women in tuxedos and evening wraps come to enjoy the unnatural thrill of pleasure and gayety in the midst of poverty and despair.

The *Walnut Grove* was the foremost of these so-called "clubs." And at the very time when the bloody massacre was occurring six miles to the south, the *Walnut Grove* was beginning to come to life for the night.

Within, a high-priced orchestra was playing slow, languorous music. Outside, the doorman, exotically attired like a Roman Legionnaire, in metal breastplate and helmet, was opening taxi doors as fast as he could for the pleasure-bent couples were arriving thick and fast.

Occasionally, however, cars arrived which disgorged sober, tight-mouthed men who were very manifestly not bent on pleasure. Their faces were hard: they were furtive in their movements, alert as prowling cougars. These men would whisper a word or two in the doorman's ear, and he would bow to them, half fearfully, and conduct them inside.

About fifty feet away from the entrance, near the corner, a freckle-faced boy stood, keenly observing the arrivals. He was no more than fifteen or sixteen, but the wide space between his clear eyes, the sensitive curve of his mouth, bespoke an intelligence higher than ordinary.

He had been there about twenty minutes now when he noted a high-powered, silent-running roadster which snaked into a vacant space at the curb close to the corner. At sight of the young man who was driving the roadster, the boy's eyes lighted up in glad recognition. But he did not rush over and utter the greeting that was on his lips. Instead, he allowed his shoulders to droop, lowered his eyes, and shuffled over to the roadster. He said in a nasal, whining voice: "Kin I watch yer car fer you, mister?"

The young man was getting out. He was revealed as tall, well-knit, with an overcoat padded at the shoulders and wasp-fitting at the waist. It was the type of coat worn by many of the swaggering gunmen and underworld czars of the city. Under his left armpit there was a readily distinguishable bulge. A three-carat diamond sparkled in his shirt front. He spoke loud, in a harsh, grating voice: "Okay, kid. You stick wit' this bus till I come out. An' you better stick wit' it, I mean!"

The boy said: "Okay, mister. Thanks."

THE YOUNG man raised the windows of the roadster's convertible top, and fumbled with the key, locking the door. As he did so, he spoke under his breath, so that none of the idlers near the corner could hear him.

"What do you think of my get-up, Tim?"

"It's a knockout, Jimmy," the boy whispered. "Where did you get the coat and the sparkler? What are you supposed to be—an actor or something?"

"I'm supposed to be a very tough gunman from Chicago, Tim. My name for tonight is Dave Orlando. Now quick—whom did you see go in the *Walnut Grove?* Did you recognize any of the faces from the rogues' gallery pictures?"

"I did, Jimmy. I recognized three of them. Tony Varro, 'Black'

Price, and Sam Selzo. There was one more I didn't recognize. The doorman took each of them inside personally."

The young man's lips tightened. "They're all on the public-enemy list, Tim. The G-Men would give their right hands to nail any one of them!"

"Shall I phone them, Jimmy?"

"No, Tim! I'm after bigger fish than those boys tonight. All you do is watch this car."

The young man finished locking up, and turned away. He strode toward the entrance of the *Walnut Grove*, whispered a word to the doorman, and was led inside.

The boy's gaze followed the young man until he disappeared. Between those two there was a strong bond of affection and admiration. The true name of the young man who had just entered the portals of the *Walnut Grove* was known to very few people. Those few—intimate friends only—knew him as Jimmy Christopher. To them, he was a warm friend who could always be counted on. To many others, though, he was a legend about whom many stories were told, and few believed. A great many people referred to him, when they spoke of him, using only the number they knew him by. And that number was—Operator 5, of the United States Intelligence Service!

The boy was known to the other agents of the service almost as well as Operator 5. Tim Donovan, the freckle-faced Irish lad who had been picked up by Operator 5 one night on New York's Lower East Side, and who had been his almost inseparable companion ever since, had acted as Jimmy Christopher's unofficial assistant in many a dangerous mission. Too young yet to be admitted to the ranks of the Intelligence Service, he nevertheless possessed nimble wit and a stalwart bravery that had more than once stood them both in good stead.

But now the boy's eyes were clouded with worry. He knew that Operator 5 was risking deadly peril in entering the *Walnut Grove* under the pseudonym of Dave Orlando. What that peril was, he could only guess. But he wished that he could share it.

Operator 5 had told him to do nothing except watch the car. He was far from satisfied with the order. His mouth quirked rebelliously, and into his eyes leaped a sparkle of mischief. He moved purposefully away from the roadster, turned the corner. There was an alley in the side street, that led into the rear of the *Walnut Grove*, right behind the kitchen....

CHAPTER 2
THE VOICE OF DOOM

INSIDE THE ornate night club, Operator 5 impatiently waved aside the mulatto hat-check girl who offered to take his coat, and allowed the doorman to conduct him past the wide entrance of the main dance floor and dining room. He cast only a single glance into its hectic interior as he followed his guide down the wide ball and up a short flight of stairs.

At a door on the upper floor, the man rapped twice, then once. Almost at once the door was thrown open by a slender woman in a black velvet evening gown that was tied high at her neck. She wore no jewelry at all, and she needed none. Her black hair was drawn tightly back into a knot, setting off the finely carved perfection of her features. Her beauty was of the flawless type which suggests that its owner must be made of marble, without human feeling of any kind.

And indeed, her eyes carried out that impression. They were dark, long-lashed, shimmering pools of mystery that conveyed nothing at all of her thoughts as her red mouth curved into a smile of welcome.

She stepped aside, said in a cool, well-controlled voice: "Come in, Orlando. The others are all here." As she moved, her body swayed beneath the tight-fitting velvet in a sort of unspoken invitation.

Operator 5 returned her smile, but said nothing. He stepped into the room. At once, the woman closed the door behind him, motioned him to a chair.

There were four other men present, all seated. The room was furnished with heavy, overstuffed furniture, and an Oriental rug into which Operator 5's feet sank with each step. Only a single floor lamp furnished the illumination, leaving the corners in darkness. From one of those corners came the strains of the orchestra below, conveyed through a radio. The *Walnut Grove* broadcast every night.

The four seated men had apparently refrained, just as Jimmy had done, from leaving their coats downstairs. Though it was warm here, they had not taken them off. They sat on the edge of their chairs, obviously ill at ease, stared at Jimmy Christopher with suspicion. They also cast side-glances at each other. All of them had their hands is their coat pockets, and Jimmy could see the bulges there. These men did not trust each other, or their hostess.

The woman now stepped to the center of the room, took Jimmy's hat and deposited it on a table near the wall. Then she said: "Gentlemen, this is Dave Orlando. He is from Chicago, and from what I hear, he is just as popular with the authorities as you gentlemen are. They say he's a wonder with a gun."

Jimmy Christopher, in keeping with the part he was taking, smirked at her, and grinned. "I ain't no slouch, Cele," he said. "I guess I can handle a rod pretty good."

The others scowled. The woman went on. "I want you to meet these gentlemen. Tony Varro, Black Price, Sam Selzo, and Bing Fraser. Now that you all know each other, I'll ask you to excuse me for a few moments, while I go and tell the boss you're here."

She moved lithely and gracefully across the room, and passed through a door in the side wall which was covered with a curtain.

As soon as she was out of me room, the four men stirred and sighed. Their eyes had all followed her sinuous form avidly. Now, Bing Fraser, a stout, bald-headed man, arose and stretched. But he was careful to keep his right hand in his pocket, and not to turn his back toward the others.

Tony Varro, a thin, pinch-faced man with narrow, close-set eyes, took a cigarette from his left hand pocket, lit it with one hand.

"Does any of you lugs know what this is all about?" he asked.

The others shook their heads. Sam Selzo, who was stocky, with a twisted nose which must have been broken at one time, parted his thick lips in a mirthless grin. "I don't know any more'n you do, Varro. All I know is, this here dame, Cele Volney, contacts me in Detroit, and propositions me to come to New York an' meet her big boss. I'm leery, but she hands me fifty G's on the line, an' says that's only chicken feed to what I'll come into if I hitch up. So I comes."

VARRO, PRICE and Fraser all nodded. Operator 5 looked from one to the other. The same thing had happened to him. For six months, he had carefully built up the identity of Dave Orlando in Chicago. Through his connections with underworld hangers-on, he had been admitted to the right circles in that city and had acted out the part of a tough gunman whose rod was for hire to the highest bidder. Working through the Intelligence Service, he had caused himself to be placed on the "wanted" list of the Department of Justice for a string of manufactured crimes. Then he had sat tight. And Cele Volney had sought him out with the same proposition that she had placed before these others.

For a long time now he had suspected the existence of a gigantic conspiracy of some sort, fathered by a Midas of the underworld. He had known that killers were being recruited for some unknown purpose. And he had deliberately set himself up as bait. So far, he was successful. His fish had nibbled.

But he could not fathom the purpose behind this expensive recruiting system. The five men in this room, including himself, had been brought here at a gross expense of a quarter of a million dollars for it seemed that the same sum—fifty thousand dollars—had been paid to each as an inducement. Varro, Price, Selzo and Fraser were even at that time being hunted all over the United States. Each had more than one killing to his credit. They had all perpetrated major crimes involving murder, and merely to associate oneself with them was to court disaster. Either Cele Volney's boss was a damned fool to attempt to work with men like these; or else he was a criminal genius. Operator 5 thrilled to the thought that he was going to meet this man in a few moments.

But he was doomed to disappointment.

The curtained door opened once more, and Cele Volney came through. She left the door ajar, and pushed the curtain to one side, revealing the yawning darkness of an unlighted room beyond. At the same time, she pressed a switch in the wall, and brilliant light from a ceiling fixture flooded the room in which Operator 5 and the four gunmen stood. It was now impossible to see anything at all beyond the doorway.

Cele Volney faced the men, smiling in queer, forced fashion.

"Now, gentlemen," she said, "the Boss will talk to you. Please do not move about, or make any sudden motions. I should tell you beforehand that it would be useless for you to try to enter the next room—in case any of you should have any ideas about discovering the identity of the Boss. There is a screen of steel mesh across that doorway—it will stop a man—or a bullet."

Her eyes traveled from one to the other as she spoke, studying each of them in turn. Her glance, for some reason, rested longest on the false Dave Orlando.

"Gentlemen," she went on, "I present you to my boss—The Scarlet Baron!"

There was a startled gasp from the four gunmen. Operator 5 hid the seething excitement within him at the mention of that name. He had half-expected that the man who was to interview them was the Scarlet Baron. His body was taut as a bowstring while he faced that darkened doorway. The name the woman had just spoken had been passed from mouth to mouth in whispers throughout the underworld for many weeks now. Men had uttered it in fear, with awe. And Jimmy Christopher noted now that Varro and the others were properly impressed. Gone was their swaggering bluster of a few moments ago. Slowly, their hands drew away from their pockets. They realized that their guns would aid them little.

Cele Volney's red lips parted in a smile as she noted their reaction. She glided across the floor and switched off the radio. And almost at once, a man's voice came from the darkened room. It was very evidently disguised. Yet it carried an effect of power and self-confidence, of cool, merciless assurance. It was artificially high-pitched, rasping.

"You men are all wanted by the government! Varro! Price! Selzo! Fraser! Orlando!" Each name as he spoke it came like the lash of a whip. "You are all gunmen. Some of you have mobs of your own. Some of you are lone wolves. But all of you are fools!"

THERE WAS a pregnant silence in the lighted room as the man in the dark ceased abruptly. The gunmen shifted uneasily.

No one had ever dared to call them fools to their faces before. Ordinarily such a statement would have brought automatics into their fists in quick resentment. But this was different. For once, they felt helpless. They had permitted themselves to be lured here by a beautiful woman and the tempting bribe of fifty thousand dollars in cash. Now they faced an invisible man behind a steel wall of meshed wire.

As Cele Volney had said, their guns were no good. They knew how to shoot, how to kill; but their intellects were unequal to the task of coping with the present situation.

The man in the dark went on. "Shall I tell you why you are fools? Any man is a fool who bucks odds that are bigger than he is. How long can you go on, hunted as you are by the G-Men? A month, six months, a year. There is always an end to the trail. You'll end up like Dillinger, on a plank in the morgue; or like Barney Broon, in prison for life!"

The speaker stopped to let that sink in. Not a man there but subconsciously knew that he had spoken the truth. The cease-

JIMMY CHRISTOPHER

less, never-ending pursuit by the G-Men would sooner or later catch up with them. Barney Broon had been a bigger criminal than any of them. For three years, he had been marked down as Public Enemy Number One, but had evaded the numerous nets spread for him, had directed his vast criminal organization from a dozen hiding places. Yet the G-Men had finally caught up with him, and Barney Broon had been seat to the new federal prison off the coast of Florida for life. He had escaped Dillinger's fate, because he had come out of his hiding place with his hands in the air, blinded by tear gas. That was the best any of them could hope for in the long run. And this man had put it to them bluntly.

Tony Varro shifted uncomfortably, scratched his ear. "Hell!" he said thickly. "They won't put me in Leander Prison. Barney Broon might have been a big shot, but he didn't have no guts. Me, they won't grab me alive!"

The man in the dark snorted. "That's why you're a fool, Varro! Only a fool pits himself against a whole country—alone!"

Jimmy Christopher's keen mind was working swiftly. He knew, of course, that there was something definite behind this deliberate attempt of the Scarlet Baron to goad them on. He saw that Cele Volney was watching them all closely, her lips parted with sharp interest, one white hand pressed against her breast. For a fleeting instant his eye caught hers, and he thought he detected a flicker in them. Was it a signal? He looked away from her, cleared his throat. Whatever the game was, it was his business to convince this Scarlet Baron that he was of different stuff from these slow-witted gunmen.

He stared straight into the darkened doorway, said softly: "Everything you say is true, Mr. Scarlet Baron. But was it worth a quarter of a million dollars to you to get us together here so you could tell us we're fools?"

The Scarlet Baron chuckled. "I just want to be sure you all understand, Orlando. You see, I have something to offer you. How would you men like to be able to walk the streets again without being hunted? How would you like it not to have a price on your heads any more?"

There was a short, startled silence among them. Then suddenly, Black Price laughed. He was a huge, hairy man, with a chest that puffed out his vest, and shoulders like an ox. His laughter bellowed through the room. He was a Pole who had once worked in the flour mills of Minnesota. He had organized crooked labor unions throughout the Middle West, had exacted graft from employers in a dozen states until he had been indicted by a Federal Grand Jury on a charge of income tax evasion. Then, seeing how they had treated Barney Broon and others, he had disappeared rather than face trial. He had recruited a dozen of his union gunmen, and had terrorized the Middle West for almost a year now. He was rapidly approaching the head of the public enemy list.

"You talk fairy tales!" he bellowed. "Neffer vill dey stop to hunt me—only ven I be dead! Now I say dat *you* are a fool!"

Tony Varro grinned, showing two rows of uneven, discolored teeth. "Price is right. Them G-boys never quit—damn 'em!"

The voice of the Scarlet Baron came to them again, very low. "Suppose I tell you that in a month there won't be any more G-Men? Suppose I tell you that in a month *I* will be the law of the land!"

JIMMY CHRISTOPHER'S eyes narrowed. Now he was coming closer to the thing that he had been trailing for months.

This was the reward of the elaborate play-acting he had gone through in Chicago to build up the identity of Dave Orlando. He glanced sideways for a moment, to catch Cele Volney's eyes on him. She had been watching him all the time.

Bing Fraser, who had remained seated, exhaled his breath deeply at the startling suggestion of the Scarlet Baron. His face assumed a pasty hue.

"The guy's nuts!" he breathed. He said it very low, almost under his breath. But the man in the next room had caught it.

"No, my friend, I am not 'nuts.' Before the evening is over, I will prove to you that I can do what I say. Now, if I can show you the way to safety—if I can take you out of the class of hunted men—what will you do in return?"

Tony Varro said earnestly: "Gee, mister, if you could do that, I'd kill a million cops for you. I'd do anything you say!"

"Would you swear to be my man—to follow wherever I lead you? Would you swear to obey me unquestioningly?"

"I would!"

"Price! What about you?"

"I be your man if you do dat, boss!"

"And you, Selzo?"

"I dunno who you are, boss, but I'll take orders from any guy can do what you say you can."

"Fraser! How do you feel about it?"

Fraser moved uncomfortably. His small eyes peered ineffectually against the darkness. "I don't see how you can do it. I think you're nuts."

From the next room the soft voice of the Scarlet Baron

purred. "You have said that once too often, Fraser. I don't like it. And I don't think you are the man for me. So—"

There was a small, wicked *spat,* accompanied by a stab of flame from the doorway. A round, black hole suddenly appeared in Fraser's forehead. He uttered a single-choked gasp that

ended in a rattle. His body wobbled, toppled to the floor. He lay still, in a curled heap. A thin trickle of blood dribbled from the hole between his eyes. He was dead.

Varro, Price and Selzo stood transfixed. They had seen death many times, had themselves killed often, without a qualm. But they had never witnessed quite so cold-blooded a murder. Their faces were strained, white. For once, they knew fear....

Cele Volney had not moved from her position beside the radio. Only, Jimmy Christopher noted that the hand at her breast clenched spasmodically, and her red, parted lips closed tightly. Her eyes showed nothing.

Jimmy himself cast not a single glance at the dead man. His eyes swiveled from the woman, sought the spot in the darkness whence the stab of name had come. There would be an opening there of some sort....

But the Scarlet Baron spoke again, still softly, without a tremor. "Please don't think that Cele lied about the mesh screen. I shot through a small opening, which is now closed again. It would be useless for any of you to attempt anything."

Varro's high-pitched voice startled them. "Ha—ha! Why should we? Fraser was no good anyway."

"I don't like to be insulted," the Scarlet Baron went on. "Let him lie there. He will be disposed of in due time. And now—" the soft purr returned—"there remains only you, Orlando. What do *you* say to my little proposition?"

Operator 5 stood taut, every muscle of his body flexed, ready for action. The others watched him like anatomy students in a clinic, observing an operation. Only Cele Volney moved slightly, raised a hand as if she would warn him in some way.

Jimmy spoke slowly. "Anybody can shoot down a defenseless man from behind a steel screen, Baron. That doesn't prove dat you can do all you say. I should like to see some other proof of your power before I commit myself. You say dat you can destroy all the G-Men. Can you bring them all into this room and shoot them down from the darkness?"

When he finished talking, a pin could have been heard dropping in that room. Not a person present dared to breathe. They expected again the wicked *spat* that had accompanied the swift doom of Fraser. Varro, Price and Selzo stared in hypnotized fascination at the strip of darkness, awaiting the spurt of flame. **BUT JIMMY CHRISTOPHER** had gauged his man well. Many a time had his fate rested on his keen judgment of human nature. His words had been carefully chosen. He had said the one thing that might avert the swift doom of that silenced gun. For to kill him now would afford no satisfaction to the Scarlet Baron. Yet, the man might be cold-blooded enough to slay again. In the split-second of silence that followed Jimmy's short speech, there came no sound from the darkened room. And then, abruptly, the Scarlet Baron chuckled.

A deep sigh came from the throats of the three gunmen. Slowly, Cele Volney's stiffened fingers unclenched at her breast. And the taut muscles of Jimmy Christopher's body relaxed slightly. He had gambled his life on his appraisal of human nature—and he had won!

The Baron was speaking. "You are a very brave man, Orlando. Braver than average. It would be a shame to kill you. You can be useful to me. I shall prove to you that I can do everything I say. Then, perhaps, you will fall in line." His voice rose a little: "Cele! What time is it?"

She responded a bit shakily: "Ten forty-five."

"Then we should be just in time for the news. Tune in on WELG. Get their news broadcast."

She obeyed, her fingers fumbling the dial. In a moment the announcer's voice came to them: "… the most dreadful crime in the nation's history! Fifteen minutes ago, down in Greenwich Village, fifty-one agents of the Federal Bureau of Investigation of the Department of Justice were massacred in a trap laid for them by the Scarlet Baron. Only one of the agents survived the carnage. The G-Men, under Ron Murdoch, veteran F.B.I. man, had planned elaborately to trap the Scarlet Baron and his gang. But they themselves fell into a trap. Mazzoli's restaurant, just off Seventh Avenue was the scene of the massacre. Our reports are sketchy just yet, but as they come in I will give you the details. It is needless to say that every agency of the government will now be focused on the job of getting the Scarlet Baron. It is war between him and the G-Men! There…."

The Scarlet Baron's voice crackled from the next room. "All right, Cele, turn it off!"

She clicked the dial, and the announcer's voice faded into silence. Jimmy Christopher's face was white, his mouth a tight, thin line. He had known Ron Murdoch well. Likewise, he had known many of the men on his staff—many of those who had been butchered down there. And behind that screen of darkness stood the man who had engineered it. His brain was seething, his blood running hot; yet his face showed nothing of his emotion.

The others, however, were gasping their admiration. "Say, Baron!" Varro exclaimed. "You got the goods! I'm stringin' wit' you! Imagine that—fifty-one G-Men at a crack!"

"Me, too, boss!" Black Price echoed. "I guess you are der Big Shot!"

Sam Selzo smirked. He raised his voice in a low chant, off key, parodying the oath to the flag: *"I pledge allegiance,"* he sang in a cracked voice, *"to the—Scarlet Baron!"*

"And you, Orlando?" the Scarlet Baron demanded. "Are you convinced now?"

"I'm convinced—Boss!" Operator 5 said through dry lips. "I'm convinced."

Not one of them even glanced at the rapidly stiffening body of Bing Fraser at their feet.

CHAPTER 3
THE MARK OF THE BARON

" I N THAT case—" the Scarlet Baron's voice sounded smug with satisfaction—"we can go on with the business of this meeting. I have proved to you four men that I can take care of the G-Men—whom you all fear like poison. That alone should recommend me to you. But there is something more— something that I have only hinted to you so far. If you think that my purpose is to establish a gang of criminals, you are mistaken. I am a very ambitious man. I have unlimited money, and I know where and how to get more whenever I need it. My ambition is *to take over the government of the United States!*"

The man in the dark paused to let that last amazing statement sink in. His listeners did not move. Three of them were mentally dazzled by the bald announcement. They could barely grasp its significance. Though they had all achieved notorious positions in the criminal world, they had never even envisioned such a possibility as the Scarlet Baron's words placed before them.

To Operator 5, though, those words were a confirmation of the suspicions he had harbored for months. He waited tensely for the Baron to go on.

"I have chosen you four men, together with a number of others who have already been interviewed, to act as my lieu- tenants. Within a month, if all my plans succeed, I will be the master of this country. You will no longer be hunted men. How does that appeal to you?"

41

Operator 5's automatic blazed and the two gunmen dropped!

Tony Varro wet his lips. "H-how you gonna get away wit' a stunt like that, Baron?"

"You'll have to take my word for it that I can do it. I trust no one with my plans. You will each have work assigned to you, and will obey your orders to the letter. If you fail, you die. If you succeed, the reward will be great. Do you all agree to enter my service?"

One after the other they nodded. Operator 5 inclined his head, too. He was convinced that the Scarlet Baron could achieve the end he boasted. A man clever and daring enough to have planned a wholesale massacre of F.B.I. men was capable of building a revolution. This was Jimmy Christopher's chance to work on the inside of the conspiracy.

The Scarlet Baron was speaking again: "Every man who enters my service must bear my mark. Cele Volney will apply it. All right, Cele."

Cele Volney stepped away from the radio, picked up from the table upon which she had deposited the hats a long instrument resembling a hypodermic syringe. To one end of it was attached an electric cord, which she plugged into a socket in the wall. At once, a peculiar, whirring sound emanated from the instrument.

The Baron's voice issued instructions. "You will take off your coats, and open your shirts. That instrument is an electric tattoo-ing machine. The mark is placed just below your left armpit. It is the initial 'B,' and serves as my signature. It identifies anyone bearing it as being in my service."

Operator 5 and the three gunmen glanced with interest at the queer instrument in Cele Volney's hand. She nodded to Tony Varro. "Do you want to be first?"

Varro hesitated a moment, asked sheepishly: "Does it hurt?"

She smiled. "A little. But it soon passes. See, I have one myself."

She raised her bare left arm, revealing a small letter "B" just beneath the armpit. Her white skin contrasted sharply with the flaming scarlet at the spot where the "B" had been seared into her flesh.

Varro shrugged. "If you can take it, lady, I can."

He removed his overcoat and jacket, and opened his shirt, raising his left arm. She moved close to him with the whirring tattoo machine, pressed the glowing end against his skin. He winced, but stood firm. She held the machine in place for perhaps a minute, then drew it away. They saw the raw, inflamed flesh under his armpit, in the shape of a "B."

Varro grinned sickishly, and buttoned his shirt. "Boy, that was hot!" he exclaimed.

Cele Volney passed from him to Black Price and Sam Selzo, whom she tattooed in turn. But when she faced Jimmy Christopher, he shook his head.

"I'm sorry," he said. "But I'll wear no man's mark!"

CELE WAS facing him squarely, with her back to the dark doorway. The Baron could not see her face. Her eyes widened, and her lips moved in mute appeal to Jimmy Christopher. She was about to whisper something to him, when the Baron's voice cracked out like a lash.

"Then you die, Orlando! Cele! Stand aside!"

Reluctantly, her hands trembling, she moved away, leaving a clear path between Jimmy Christopher and that dark doorway. Varro, Price and Selzo looked at him pityingly.

Jimmy Christopher had already taken stock of the room. He had noted something that had perhaps escaped the attention of the Scarlet Baron even—namely, that the corner of the room where Cele Volney had stood, next to the radio, was out of line with that doorway. A man standing there would be safe from the hidden gun. And just as Cele Volney stepped aside, he launched himself in a desperate leap toward that corner, while at the same time his right hand streaked to his shoulder holster, appearing with his automatic.

Flame lanced from the darkness, but Jimmy had moved too fast. A slug thudded into the wall behind him. His body was in motion, and he raised his automatic, seat a bullet at the spot whence the flame had come. But the Scarlet Baron had acted quickly, too, had closed the opening through which he had fired.

Jimmy's slug clanged against steel. The roar of his gun filled the room, as his hurtling body struck the radio, sent it crashing to the floor. He swiveled, his back to the wall, swinging the automatic to cover the three gunmen. Black Price, slow-witted, was standing spraddle-legged in the middle of the room, near the prone body of Bing Fraser. He was gazing dazedly at the smashed radio.

But Varro and Sam Selzo were quicker to grasp the situation. This was their opportunity to prove their worth to their new boss. And they seized it with fierce satisfaction. They went for their guns with the swift motions of expert killers. But

Operator 5's automatic blazed twice again, before they could shoot. The two gunmen were hurled backward as by an invisible force, crumpled to the floor, each with a bullet in his heart.

Through the smoke, Jimmy Christopher saw the huge figure of Black Price, still standing, dazed, in the middle of the room. But of Cele Volney there was no sign. She had disappeared.

Operator 5 shouted: "Stand still, Price, or I'll give it to you!" He moved forward, drew a small but powerful pencil flashlight from his pocket, and threw its beam into the next room. The long finger of light showed him a small room, empty of furniture, with a steel screen door swinging open. The Baron must have opened it for Cele Volney to pass through. And they had both probably made their escape through a back passage, knowing that the shots would bring police shortly.

Jimmy Christopher smiled bitterly. He had failed. All his work of the past months was wasted—because he had stubbornly refused to have a little letter tattooed upon him. There was a reason for that, though, which went deeper than personal vanity. He had watched carefully the tattooing of the three gunmen; he had noticed in each case that Cele Volney had seemed to press on the top of the instrument just before she removed it. That pressure, with her thumb, appeared to be unnecessary to the tattooing.

Now, while he kept Black Price covered, he stooped and picked up the instrument the woman had dropped. The wire was still plugged into the socket, and the letter "B" was still glowing red hot. While Price watched, crouching, waiting for a chance to jump him, Jimmy Christopher applied the pressure of his thumb just as he had seen Cele do. And he nodded to himself. For a hypodermic needle lanced out from the center of the glowing metal, then snapped in again.

His surmise had been correct. The Baron's purpose in branding his followers was not alone to identify them. Under cover of the operation he was able to inject into their systems some kind of drug without their knowledge. What that drug was would soon be ascertained when Jimmy got the thing into his private laboratory. Now he pulled the electric cord from the socket, waited while the glow subsided. He stared at Black Price, whose hands were clenched into huge knots, and whose eyes were showing little red spots in the corners.

"Well," he asked the big man, "what do you think of your Baron now?"

Price swallowed hard. "Vat you gonna do vit' me?" he demanded. "Who in hell are you, anyvay?"

Jimmy smiled enigmatically. "You'll have plenty of time to find out—in jail. Maybe it's a good thing for you that you'll be in jail. If my guess is right, there's going to be a lot of trouble in this country—starting pretty soon!"

Shouting, and the sound of police whistles came to them from below. Feet pounded on the stairway. The police had arrived. They burst through the door and Jimmy exhibited to the police credentials showing that he was George Wakely of the Department of Justice. He used those credentials whenever it was necessary to establish himself with the local police authorities. It saved him from the necessity of revealing himself as Operator 5.

He turned his prisoner over to the lieutenant who shortly appeared on the scene, and himself directed a thorough search of the premises of the *Walnut Grove*. But there was no trace of the Scarlet Baron, or of Cele Volney.

While the police were searching, he went out to look for Tim Donovan, and his forehead creased in a frown when he could not locate the boy. His roadster was still at the curb where he had left it, and he sought for a note which Tim might possibly have left. But there was none. For some inexplicable reason, the lad had left.

OPERATOR 5 walked down the narrow alley toward the kitchen, and saw two bluecoats stooping over an inert form on the ground. His heart skipped a beat, and he hastened toward them, but breathed in relief when he found that the unconscious form was not that of Tim Donovan, but of a thin man. The man had been struck a hard blow on the back of his skull. Near him lay an automatic with blood on the butt.

"I think I know this guy, sir," one of the bluecoats told him. "It's Chet Sweeney. He's wanted for jumpin' bail on a felony charge."

Jimmy Christopher nodded. He bent, pulled back the unconscious man's overcoat and jacket, ripped away his shirt at the armpit, revealing a bright red letter "B" tattooed under the arm.

The cops gasped.

"Take him down to the precinct house," Jimmy ordered. "Have him treated there instead of at a hospital. And keep a guard with him every minute. I want to talk to that man when he comes to!"

Jimmy Christopher then returned to the interior of the *Walnut Grove*, where each guest was being closely questioned, compelled to prove his identity and residence before being allowed to depart. The manager of the club, as well as all the employees, was taken into custody, held for further examination. They were being loaded into a patrol wagon together with Black Price.

Operator 5 looked into the room where the guests were being questioned, saw that a police captain and a deputy commissioner, whom he knew by sight, had arrived to take charge.

He heard the captain say to the commissioner: "I phoned the Department of Justice, sir. They're pretty well disorganized by that massacre downtown, but they're sending a couple of men up here right away. The man who answered the phone doesn't know this George Wakely, but figures he might be working directly out of Washington. He'll—"

Jimmy Christopher waited to hear no more. He about-faced and walked out of the building. At this time, he did not want to have to explain to the Department of Justice men just who he was. The police were capable of holding the place down till the F.B.I. men arrived. There was nothing he could do here now, for he was pretty sure that the Scarlet Baron had escaped. The questioning of the man who had been found in the alley could be taken care of by the police or the Justice men. There were other things that he wanted to do.

Outside, he looked around once more for Tim, and failed to see him. Glumly, he got into his car and drove away. It wasn't like Tim to desert a post that way. Something vital must have come up....

CHAPTER 4
PRAISE FOR A TRAITOR

WHEN TIM DONOVAN drifted into the alley behind the *Walnut Grove*, his whole bearing became subconsciously alert and watchful. He knew that he was disobeying orders. And he didn't want to do anything that would embarrass Jimmy Christopher, or interfere with his plans. Yet he wanted to be in the action—if there was any.

In spite of his watchfulness, however, he did not notice the dark form of the thin man, who stepped back into the shadows when Tim appeared. The boy stepped carefully, making his way toward a slit of light that fell from the partly open kitchen door of the night club. The clank of pots and pans came to him from the lighted kitchen, as well as the raucous voices of the waiters, calling out their orders to the chef.

He raised his eyes, saw a lighted window directly above the kitchen. He was about to move further along the alley, when a figure detached itself suddenly from the shadows, sprang forward and seized his arm in a cruel grip.

"What you doin' here, kid?" a sharp voice demanded.

Tim, startled, peered at the narrow, pinched face close to his own in the darkness, at the eyes brittle with suspicion. This man was a lookout of some sort, and he had blundered right into him. He thought ruefully that he had put his foot in it this time.

His arm hurt under the man's tight fingers, but he did not try to squirm out of the grip. He saw that his captor's other hand was in a coat pocket, knew that he was probably holding a gun or blackjack there.

The boy assumed the whining tone that he had used outside when speaking to Jimmy Christopher. "Geez, mister," he said, "I ain't done nothin' I'm hungry, an' I was lookin' fer somethin' to eat I thought maybe if I washed some dishes for the chef, he'd gimme a handout."

The other's attitude of sharp suspicion did not relax. "That's why you was creepin' in here on the sly, huh? Come on—" he twisted the boy's arm so that Tim gasped with the sudden pain—"talk up. What was you—?"

The thin man stopped suddenly as Tim wilted, allowed his slight body to sag. "Cripes! He's fainted!" Tim heard the man mutter. The lad felt his captor's grip on his arm relax, and he let his body stretch full length on the cold, slushy pavement.

The lookout cursed softly to himself, and bent over the supposedly unconscious waif. He said softly: "You ain't sham-min' by any chance, are you?" His hand came out of his pocket with a gleaming, gun-metal automatic, and he raked the sight sharply across Tim's face from the right cheek-bone down to his mouth, drawing blood.

The boy stiffened, forced himself to lie still, although the pain of the cut sent prickles of agony across his eyes. The man grunted, started to straighten up. And Tim's legs shot out, caught the other's ankles in a scissors hold. Then he twisted himself sharply, setting his whole body as a fulcrum against the man's legs. The thin man gasped, went toppling over, clawing at the air to recover his balance.

It was a trick that Jimmy Christopher had taught to the lad, among many other secrets of rough-and-tumble fighting. Any one of those tricks, if judiciously used, would make a mere boy the superior over a grown, powerful man.

The lookout struck the ground with his hands outstretched to break his fall; and in doing so he let go of the automatic. Tim squirmed around, seized it by the barrel and brought the butt down hard on the back of the man's skull. The other's breath escaped in a long wheeze, and he plumped down on his face.

TIM SCRAMBLED to his feet. The butt of the automatic felt wet and sticky. He hastily tugged at the unconscious man, dragged him into the shadow. And just then there sounded from upstairs the report of an automatic. Tim looked up, startled. The shot had seemed to come from the room directly above the kitchen, where he had seen the light. Immediately after it, there came two more staccato reports in quick succession—so quick that they sounded almost as one.

Tim's eyes shone eagerly in the darkness. He guessed that Jimmy Christopher was up there. He glanced along the rear wall of the building, seeking some means of getting up to that first-floor room.

And white he was looking, a section of the back wall about

ten feet from the kitchen entrance swung open, and a man and a woman emerged. The man's collar was turned up, his hat pulled low over his face. The woman wore a dark fur coat with a high collar which almost entirely concealed her face.

As Tim watched, the opening in the wall swung shut behind them, and they saw Tim's shadowy figure in the alley. The man called out softly: "Sweeney! That you?"

Tim could see the sheen of a gun in the man's hand. He grunted, as he had heard the lookout do, refrained from talking.

The man said hurriedly; "Hell's broke loose upstairs. There's a copper up there, posing as Dave Orlando. I'm going through to the car, on the back street. You cover us."

As he spoke, the man fitted a key into the door of the building adjoining the night dab, directly across the alley. He was turned slightly away from Tim, and the boy exclaimed: "You're not going anywhere, mister! Put your hands up!" At the same time he took a step forward, thrusting Sweeney's automatic out at the man with the key.

But his fortune was not to last. That forward step was a mistake. He stumbled over the body of Sweeney, and before he could recover his balance, the man with the key had swung around, raised his gun, and brought it down on Tim's head. The boy fell, unconscious, across the body of the lookout.

The woman, who had been silent, said huskily: "This boy must be with Orlando—"

"Yes!" the man rasped. "And this is our chance to find out who Orlando really is. If this kid knows, we'll get it out of him! Here, Cele—" he thrust a key into her hand—"get that door open!"

He stooped and raised Tim's form to his shoulder, then hurried through into the passageway which Cele Volney had opened. The door shut behind them. The alley was silent again, with the still, unconscious figure of Sweeney, lying in the shadow.

From the front of the *Walnut Grove* came the sounds of police whistles and radio car sirens. People were shouting in excitement. But no one came out of the kitchen to see what was happening in the alley. Apparently the employees of the *Walnut Grove* attended strictly to their own business.

IT WAS less than two hours later that Jimmy Christopher sat in the office of United States Intelligence. Z-7 was drumming once again, rapidly, on the glass top of his desk. Two other men were there. One was John Hobson, the assistant director of the Federal Bureau of Investigation, who bad flown from Washington that afternoon. The other was Sigmund Paulson, the only survivor of the massacre at Greenwich Village.

Hobson's face was gray and drawn. He was talking earnestly, emphatically. "I was at the White House this afternoon, Z-7. The President talked to me for twenty minutes. He instructed me to contact you here in New York, and enlist the services of the Intelligence. This thing has gone beyond the scope of the Federal Bureau of Investigation. The whole country is demoralized. This Scarlet Baron must have a tremendous organization. He plans two or three *coup*s to take place at one time, in various parts of the United States. While his men were mowing down our agents in Greenwich Village, a trans-continental train was wrecked near Kansas City, and a newspaper plant was bombed in Boston. I can't understand what his purpose is. There was no profit in either of those crimes. And he certainly could gain nothing from the massacre of my men tonight. All he has accomplished is to bring  the whole nation after him. He must have realized, when he planned that trap at Mazzoli's, that we will never rest until those fifty-one men are avenged. Why should he deliberately bring the whole power of the United States after him—?"

"I think I can answer that, sir," Jimmy Christopher broke in quietly. "I actually talked to the Scarlet Baron tonight. He partially revealed his plans. He is planning nothing less than—a revolution!"

Hobson gasped. Z-7 looked quizzically at Operator 5, while Sigmund Paulson stirred uncomfortably in his seat, and lowered his eyes. Paulson had been admitted to this conference because he was regarded as a sort of hero, being the only survivor of the massacre. Hobson had promoted him to the position held by the slain Murdoch, and Paulson was now in command of all the agents being rushed to the New York area from all parts of the country.

Hobson laughed nervously at Jimmy Christopher's statement. "That's a little wild, don't you think, Operator 5? I'll admit that the Scarlet Baron controls the most powerful criminal organization since Barney Broon was put in jail. But he hardly rates the status of a revolutionary leader. We—"

He paused as a knock sounded on the door. A shirt-sleeved

agent from the outer room entered, white-faced, with a sheet of paper to which were pasted bits of ticker tape. He thrust the sheet at Z-7.

"This just came over the teletype, sir!" he blurted. "It's from our Philadelphia headquarters. There's hell to pay over there!"

Z-7 seized the sheet, glanced through it rapidly, his jaw hardening as he read. When he finished he passed it to Operator 5. "There's confirmation of what you've just been saying, Jimmy!"

The message read:

Z-7... MW-NY... ROUTE THROUGH WDC-13... RIOTS SPREADING INSTREETS OF PHILADELPHIA... POLICE OVERWHELMED BY SUPERIOR NUMBERS... RIOTERS ARMED WITH MODERN WEAPONS... HAND-TO-HAND FIGHTING IN INDEPENDENCE SQUARE... MOB BESIEGING CITY HALL... MAYOR ASKING FOR MILITIA... INCITERS OF RIOT UNKNOWN BUT MOB IS DEMANDING THAT ALL RESERVE MONEY IN TREASURY AND RE SERVE BANKS HERE BE DISTRIBUTED AMONG THEM... ARE WE AUTHORIZED TO TAKE A HAND... SITUATION VERY SERIOUS... PP-1....

Hobson had read the message over Jimmy's shoulder. He gasped: "God, you were right, Operator 5! The Scarlet Baron must be back of this. I—"

He paused as another knock sounded at the door, and the same shirt-sleeved agent entered with two more teletype messages.

Z-7 EXTENDED his hand for them wordlessly, as if he were almost afraid to learn the news they contained. His eyes widened as he read them. One was from Savannah, Georgia, the other from Des Moines, Iowa. Both contained news very similar to that in the first message from Philadelphia. He passed them on to Jimmy Christopher, then reached for the phone.

"Get me Washington!" he rapped into the instrument. He looked up at the others. "Riots in three cities! Men well armed! The Scarlet Baron is striking. God knows how many more of these messages we'll get before the night is over. By morning the whole country may well be in turmoil—!"

He swung back to the phone as he got the connection. "Bronson!" he snapped to the man in the Washington office. "Listen carefully. You've got to find the Secretary of War!" He proceeded to issue swift, terse instructions. When he had finished be cradled the telephone, turned to Jimmy and the others, "Well, by morning the National Guard will be in control. We'll nip this thing m the bud!"

Jimmy Christopher shook his head. "I'm afraid not, sir. The Scarlet Baron is no doubt expecting the national government to take just such action. Be sure that he has prepared for it. He's no fool!"

Z-7 licked his lips. "Then what do you suggest?"

Jimmy shrugged. "We've got to get every agent available on the job of identifying the Scarlet Baron. We've got to find out who he is, nail him somehow, and leave this revolution of his leaderless."

Hobson laughed bitterly. "How do you propose to do that

57

TIM DONOVAN

little thing, Operator 5? You've already tried once, and failed. You haven't got a thing to work on."

"But I have, sir. There's the man who was found unconscious

in the alley back of the *Walnut Grove*. He has a 'B' tattooed on him. He's one of the Baron's men. I'm going down to the precinct house and question him. We've simply *got* to make him talk!"

Hobson nodded. "I'll go with you. What about you, Paulson?" He turned to the tight-lipped F.B.I. man. "Want to come along?"

Paulson shook his head. "I think I better run over to our headquarters, Mr. Hobson, and take care of organizing the men who are coming in. I'll be there if you want me."

"Okay," Hobson said. The three men arose, leaving Z-7 seated at his desk. At the door, Jimmy Christopher turned, went back for a moment. "I told you about Tim Donovan, Chief," he said worriedly. "I'm afraid something's happened to—the kid. Won't you have the men keep an eye out for him?"

Z-7 nodded. "I'll instruct every one of the agents who reports in to be on the lookout for him, Jimmy. I wish that kid would keep his freckled nose out of danger!"

Jimmy reproached himself bitterly, "I should—never have asked him to meet me at the *Walnut Grove*. If anything has happened to Tim, it's my fault!"

"You couldn't help it, Jimmy," Z-7 consoled him. "And

anyway, maybe he's all right. Tim Donovan is a smart boy. He's well able to take care of himself. He'll probably surprise you by turning up when you least expect him."

"I hope you're right, Chief," Jimmy Christopher said soberly.

He left Z-7, and rode down silently with Hobson and Sigmund Paulson, in the high-speed express elevator that served the Intelligence Offices exclusively.

At the curb, Paulson left them, and Jimmy invited the F.B.I. director to ride to the precinct house in his roadster. "It's hardly likely," Hobson remarked, after saying good-bye to Paulson, and giving him some last minute instructions, "that this man, Sweeney, will know much about the Scarlet Baron. If, as you say, he was only a lookout—"

"That's all he was," Jimmy told the other, guiding the car skillfully across town, "but he may be able to furnish us with, some little clue that will put us back on the Baron's trail. That's all I want!" He would not have been so optimistic had he been able to watch Sigmund Paulson's movements as soon as they had left....

That gaunt-eyed agent hurried around the corner, peering furtively behind him to make sure that Jimmy Christopher and Hobson were not returning. He entered a small cigar store, stepped quickly into the phone booth, and dialed a number. To the voice that answered he spoke low and swiftly, his voice taking on a whining edge:

"Paulson talking. Listen, I know who Dave Orlando really is!"

"Who?" The one word crackled over the wire like the sting of a lash.

"He's really Operator 5 of the United States Intelligence

Service. And that boy you picked up tonight is Tim Donovan. He's Operator 5's friend, and assistant. Operator 5 would give his right hand to save that kid."

"So? That is good work, Paulson. You know more, perhaps? You know where I could find this Operator 5, perhaps?"

"He's gone with Hobson to the precinct house where they're holding Sweeney. He's going to get some information out of Sweeney—if he can."

"That is very interesting, Paulson. We will try to arrange a little reception for our friend Operator 5 at the precinct house. I am afraid he will be a little disappointed if he expects to talk to Sweeney." A low chuckle sounded over the phone. "You have done well—"

Paulson broke in with piteous eagerness, his white-knuckled hand clutching the telephone receiver so that it seemed that the instrument would crush under the pressure. "And can I come over for some—some—treatment? I've done everything you told me to. I've betrayed my country, my friends. Please! Can I come over?"

"Yes, Paulson, you may come. You have done very well. Come in an hour."

The voice at the other end was paternal, suave.

Paulson breathed: "Thank you! Thank you!" He hung up and walked out of the store as if treading on air. His eyes were bright with expectancy. Already he seemed to have forgotten the things that he had done, to have forgotten the brand of treachery with which he had seared his immortal soul. Just a few words from that man at the other end of the phone had raised him from morose, gaunt-eyed, hollow-cheeked despondency to a state of feverish eagerness....

CHAPTER 5
SUICIDE DETAIL

TO REACH the precinct house on Forty-seventh Street where Sweeney was being held, it was necessary to drive west across town, and then up along either Fifth or Sixth Avenue. It was merest chance that caused Jimmy Christopher, with Hobson in the roadster beside him, to choose Sixth instead of Fifth.

As he swung right into the avenue from Forty-Second Street, his eye caught the glare of the neon signs on the huge Hippodrome building up on the next corner. The blazing lights announced that a meeting of the National Wealth-Sharing Movement was being held there tonight.

Outside the big theater structure, crowds were milling about, struggling to gain admission. A four-piece brass band was playing in the lobby, its strident notes carrying out into the street above the rumble of the "L" overhead.

Suddenly, Jimmy Christopher's eyes narrowed. He applied his brake, slowed up along the curb in front of the theater. Hobson glanced at him impatiently. "Don't waste any more time than necessary, Operator 5. We've got to get Sweeney to talk—"

"Look here, sir," Jimmy objected earnestly. "I've got a hunch. This National Wealth-Sharing Movement has only begun to be well known within the last month or two. Yet they've held meetings in dozens of cities, and they seem to have unlimited funds. It must have cost them plenty, for instance, to hire the Hippodrome."

"What of it?" Hobson demanded testily. "Let's get going, man. Here we are, following up the only possible trail to the Scarlet Baron, and you stop and give me a lecture on the Wealth-Sharing Movement. I don't understand you, Operator 5. I was told that you are the ace operative of the Intelligence Service. But this wasting of time—"

"It's not a waste of time, sir. Don't you see? We're getting reports of riots all over the country. The rioters are demanding that the money in the treasury be divided among them. There's a connection, sir. I'm going to attend that meeting!"

He swung the roadster sharply in toward the curb, started to ease it into a vacant parking spot Hobson put a hand on his arm. "I won't have it. Operator 5! This is ridiculous. The most important thing for us to do right now is to interview Sweeney at the station house. I insist that you come with me!"

"I'm sorry, sir," Jimmy Christopher said quietly, "but I am not under your orders. And with the strong hunch I've got right now, I'd disobey the President himself if he ordered me to stay away from this meeting!"

Hobson stared at him wrathfully for a moment, then shrugged in resignation. "If I had a man like you in the F.B.I., Operator 5, I'd fire him out so fast he wouldn't know what was happening to him. This is a serious matter. We can't ride hunches—"

"I'm riding this one, sir!"

"All right, then you'll ride it yourself. I'm going on to the station house alone, and we'll see what Z-7 has to say about this insubordination of yours when I talk to him!"

Hobson got out of the roadster, stalked away in indignation. Jimmy Christopher started for the brilliantly lit entrance of the Hippodrome, only to stop short at sight of a young, chestnut-haired young woman who was stepping dejectedly from the lobby. She saw him at the same time that he saw her, and exclaimed delightedly: "Jimmy!"

"Diane!" he called out, as he thrust aside half a dozen men on the sidewalk to get to her. "How come you're here?" There was a warmth in his glance that seemed to find an answer in the eyes of the trimly dressed, pretty girl.

"I've been trying to get into that meeting," she pouted. "I was assigned to cover it; but they won't let me in. You have to have a pass, it seems!"

DIANE ELLIOT, star reporter for the Amalgamated Press, had known and admired Jimmy Christopher for a long time. With the boy, Tim Donovan, she was one of the few people outside the service who knew that he also was Operator 5. But Jimmy trusted her with much more than that knowledge. Often she had risked her life with him. And she looked forward wistfully to the day when Jimmy Christopher would leave forever behind him the constant perils of the service, and return to private life—perhaps to the happiness of marriage and a home, like other men.

Until the day that he felt free to retire, Jimmy had resolutely vowed to himself that he would remain without ties which might hamper his work. And Diane loved him well enough to wait.

Now he took her arm, guided her through the press of milling men around the corner on the Forty-third Street side of the Hippodrome. Here, several police officers were engaged in keeping order in a long line of men waiting for admission to the balcony through the aide entrance. Jimmy said to Diane: "Wait here just a minute, Di. I'm going to find out what this is all about."

He left her and approached one of the uniformed patrolmen. "How do you get a pass for this thing, Cap?" he asked.

The officer shrugged. "I don't know any more about it than you do, buddy. All I know is, this Wealth-Sharing Movement has a permit for the meeting, and us boys from the precinct house get the dirty end of it. I was due to go off at midnight, but I have to put in the extra time because they didn't get started till two hours after schedule. If you haven't got a pass, you better breeze."

Jimmy moved away, back toward Diane. Suddenly, he stopped, rigid. A sedan had pulled up at the curb near the stage entrance, and from it there descended a woman—Cele Volney! She was accompanied by two men, and the three hurried in through the gate, looking neither to the right or the left.

Jimmy Christopher's eyes lit up with excitement. His hunch had been a good one. He walked swiftly back to Diane, said tightly: "Di, I've got to get in there! The woman who just went in is Cele Volney—the Scarlet Baron's field-agent! You wait right here!"

Before she could protest, he left her once more, mingled with the crowd of men on the sidewalk. He saw one fellow, in a ragged overcoat and a dirty felt hat, who clutched a bit of pasteboard in his hand. Jimmy edged up alongside this man, said to him: "Say, buddy, how do you get one of those passes?"

The ragged one glanced around at him with dark, suspicious eyes, and his mouth twisted in a sneer. "You got to be poor to get one o' these, pal," he said. "There's gonna be big doings in there tonight. Them Wealth-Sharing guys are looking out for the interests of the Forgotten Man, all right!"

"Look," said Jimmy. "How would you like to sell that pass? I'll give you a dollar for it"

The man shook his head. "The guy who gave me this today said that everybody who came to the meeting would get a chance to make five grand for himself. I think he was nuts, personally, but I'll gamble the buck against the five grand."

"Suppose I make it ten?"

"A sawbuck! You'd give me a sawbuck for this pass?"

Jimmy fingered the roll of bills in his pocket, pulled one out and showed it to the other. It was a ten. "There it is!"

The man's eyes shone. "Here you are, pal! I wish I had a couple more to sell you!"

Jimmy exchanged his ten dollars for the pass, watched the seedy-looking man hurry away across the street. Ten dollars in the hand, he had figured, was better than five thousand in the bush. Jimmy pocketed his pass, moved on to another man, and negotiated the purchase of a second pass.

Then he went back and got Diane, led her into the lobby of the Hippodrome. Both passes called for orchestra seats, and they were admitted by the two men at the door without question.

INSIDE, THE place was almost filled. There were no reserved seats, and Jimmy and Diane were forced to find a place far at the rear of the orchestra.

The house was brilliantly lighted, and there was a row of chairs on the stage occupied by half a dozen men. As Jimmy and Diane were seating themselves, they saw Cele Volney and her two escorts enter from the wings, and take chairs at the end of the row on the stage. The woman appeared quite composed, apparently none the worse for her experience earlier in the evening at the *Walnut Grove.* In fact, she seemed so cool and fresh, that Jimmy almost doubted that she was the same woman who had branded Varro, Price and Selzo, only to see two of the gangsters die under his own guns.

Diane whispered to him: "Look at these men in the audience, Jimmy. They look as if they hadn't had a square meal in weeks. And some of them are really vicious-looking. The Wealth-Sharing Movement seems to be appealing to the worst elements in the city!"

Jimmy nodded. "Di, you're going to have a scoop for the Amalgamated Press. I think this is going to be the beginning of another riot like the ones in Philadelphia and Savannah and Des Moines!"

Her eyes opened wide. "Riots! What are you talking about?

67

There haven't been any riots in those cities—that I know of. And I saw the latest bulletins at the office less than a half-hour ago!"

Jimmy became thoughtful. "Listen, Di, there's something queer going on. Z-7 received teletype messages from our offices in those places, reporting riots. Those messages couldn't possibly have been faked. It means that *somebody* must be censoring all the news coming from those centers. The Scarlet Baron—"

He stopped as a man on the platform advanced to the speaker's table, rapped sharply with a gavel. A hush fell over the big place. The man spoke into a microphone, and his voice was magnified by loud speakers located throughout the house.

"Ladies and gentlemen," he called. "You are all members of the same class—the class of Forgotten Men! We of the Wealth-Sharing Movement have brought you together here tonight to show you how to come into your own. It has been written that the meek shall inherit the earth; and tonight—" his voice rose in thundering accents—*"you shall receive your inheritance!"*

As the speaker stopped, shouts, applause, catcalls and jeers greeted his strange announcement. He waited until the noise had abated, and then went on. "You may laugh now. You may think that we promise the impossible. Well, it will cost you nothing to listen. You have nothing to lose—everything to gain. You have all been kicked around for years now. Sometimes you eat, and sometimes you don't. Sometimes you have a place to sleep, and sometimes you sleep on the benches in Bryant Park, down the street. You can't even get relief, because you have no homes. And those of you who have homes are subjected to every humiliation when you go to get the little, miserable doles that are handed out to you. You have to be investigated; you have to answer a thousand questions; you have to stand in line for hours. And then what do you get?"

He paused, as if expecting an answer to his rhetorical question. There were a few isolated boos here and there, but several voices along the aisles shouted: "Let the man talk! He's right!"

The boos were silenced.

Jimmy whispered to Diane: "He's got his own men planted in the audience. They're going to swing these people in his favor!"

Diane nodded wordlessly, her eyes on the speaker, who had resumed: "You get a miserable food ticket. You go to a store that makes a profit on the food it gives you in exchange for that ticket. The store makes a profit, the big packers make a profit, the railroad company that transported that food makes a profit— and all the politicians make a profit out of your misery! And yet they slaughter hogs out west, and plough under fields of grain and corn. Men, I tell you that there is enough wealth in this country to make every one of us a millionaire!"

HE STOPPED, and there was a burst of cheering from the stooges along the aisles, which was taken up immediately by the rest of the audience. Soon the whole house rocked to thunderous applause.

The speaker raised a hand for silence, and when the applause had subsided, he continued: "Why should we starve amid plenty? Why should we come begging for that which is our right? Let us take what's really ours!"

Jimmy Christopher had been watching the uniformed police-

69

men, of whom there were about fifty scattered about the house. Now, at the speaker's words, a sergeant who stood in the aisle near where Jimmy and Diane were seated, frowned, and started down toward the stage.

The speaker shouted into the microphone: "Men, tonight we shall take what belongs to us. No longer will we ask for favors. From tonight on, we shall know hunger no more. We shall follow a new leader—one who will pour wealth and plenty into our laps. And those who try to stop us shall die!"

The police sergeant who was half-way down the aisle, shouted: "Stop! You are under arrest!" He drew his service revolver, ran forward. The bluecoats in the aisles also started toward the stage, at a wave of his arm.

The speaker did not appear to be disturbed, however. He raised his hand, pointed at the sergeant, and thundered into the microphone: "I said that those who oppose us shall die. *Now!*"

As if his word had been a signal, men suddenly appeared on the stage, from either wing, armed with sub-machine guns. Each one was sure of himself, apparently having been carefully coached what to do.

They knelt, raised the sub-machine guns, and directed a withering, roaring hail of lead along the aisles at the advancing police. The bluecoats were mowed down without firing a shot. The staccato thunder of the guns filled the huge theater with deafening sound and with the acrid fumes of powder. In less than a minute, the machine-guns ceased firing; the gunners rose to their feet, swung their weapons in wide arcs to cover the audience.

Along all the aisles men had arisen, armed with automatics.

Shots were fired at isolated bluecoats who had escaped the first barrage from the stage.

The whole house was in pandemonium. No one was seated any longer. Men and women had risen to their feet, shouting, screaming, raving. Some were paralyzed with fear. Others streamed in fierce exultation at the sudden orgy of wealth that had been promised them, and at this obvious beginning of the speaker's lavish promises. Fights started in fifty spots.

Jimmy Christopher's hand had streaked to his armpit at the first shot fired from the stage. His automatic was out when Diane gripped his arm, shouted frenziedly in his ear above the bursting thunder of the guns:

"No, no, Jimmy! You can't do any good! You'll only get yourself killed. Wait, Jimmy!" She dragged his wrist down, so that the gun was out of sight.

And then it was over.

The house was in the control of the speaker's gunmen. The machine gunners on the stage menaced the audience, while the plug-uglies with automatics kept the crowd from spilling out into the aisles.

The magnifiers carried the speaker's voice: "Quiet! Quiet, everybody! Anybody who wants it can have the same dose of lead!"

The first panic subsided. Men and women sank into their seats, anxious to avoid the murderous gaze of the gunmen in the aisles.

The speaker announced: "That's what's going to happen to our opposition everywhere! Our leader is a man of action. He is going to give everybody enough to eat. He is going to redistribute the wealth of the country. Be quiet, everybody. He's going to talk to you now! Ladies and gentlemen, listen to—the *Starlet Baton!*"

THAT ANNOUNCEMENT brought a hush to the house, deeper than the threat of death. The Scarlet Baron! These people had all read about the Scarlet Baron's exploits. They knew that he had done the impossible time and again. If he was behind this thing, then it had every chance of success. In that crowd, there were many who were revolted by the sudden, merciless slaughter of the bluecoats in the aisles. There were others who had merely come out of curiosity. But there were many who were desperate, at the end of their rope. There were many who had secretly wished that they could share in the Scarlet Baron's depredations, who had hoped for a chance to work for him. Now they had it....

In the sudden quiet that spread over the Hippodrome, a voice began to speak, out of the magnifiers. Jimmy Christopher recognized that voice. He bad heard it only a few hours ago, at the *Walnut Grove.* The Scarlet Baron was somewhere backstage, talking into another microphone.

"You have all heard of me," he said suavely. "You think of me as a criminal, because I kill—just as I killed these oxen in uniforms. But whom do I kill? You know the answer. I make war on those who keep you poor, I kill those who work for the system that takes all the wealth and gives you the crumbs. I am not a criminal. George Washington was no criminal, yet he killed those who oppressed. Lincoln was no criminal, yet he killed those who would have kept human beings as slaves. In

72

every land, in every age, there have been those who fought for the common people against their masters. I am one of those. Will you help me fight your fight? Will you help me to take the wealth of this country and divide it among you? I will lead you to victory and to wealth. Will you follow me?"

The Baron ceased talking, and there was a full minute of vibrant silence. Then, like an avalanche, the roar of a thousand frenzied voices rolled toward the stage from the hoarse throats of the audience. They were carried away with excitement and lust for wealth. The shooting which had just occurred served to destroy their sense of values; now this sudden offer of determined leadership swept them off their feet. The din of shouting and applause smashed against the eardrums of Jimmy Christopher and Diane Elliot, almost drowning out the sounds of gunfire from the street outside. Some sort of battle was being waged out there, too.

Jimmy could guess what it was. The Baron had no doubt planted other men with machine guns to take care of any reinforcements which might arrive for the police. There was little question as to who would be victorious. The Scarlet Baron had planned far too well.

Now, as the Baron's voice sounded again through the magnifiers, the noise died away. They were all anxious, eager to hear more.

"I thank you all, my friends! You will live to bless the day that the Scarlet Baron came to lead you! We will never stop now, till we are the masters of the land. You will all be given arms. And we shall march downtown. In an hour the city will be ours. This same thing is happening all over the country. Tomorrow there will be no law in the land but that of the Scarlet Baron! And my law will be the law of the people! You shall share in the wealth that has been accumulated as a result of your misery. All right! Distribute the arms!"

At once, men began to wheel huge boxes, on hand trucks, onto the stage. From the boxes they took armfuls of rifles, gave them to other men who went up the aisles with them, passing them into the eager, grasping hands of those in the audience.

The speaker on the platform raised his arms, and called into the microphone: "Keep your seats, everybody! When you are all armed, we will march out. Follow your leaders—the men with the red armbands. They will tell you what to do!"

THERE HAD appeared on the sleeves of the plug-uglies in the aisles red bands upon which was painted a black letter "B." These were the men who were to lead the frenzied crowd in its search for wealth. Just so had revolutions started in many lands; revolutions that had uprooted every vestige of decency in the countries where they had taken place; revolutions that had inaugurated reigns of terror, with rivers of blood flowing through the streets. They had all, invariably, been guided by cold, calculating minds like the Scarlet Baron's. They had all plunged the blinded citizens into depths of horror and misery far worse than those they had known before.

Now the Scarlet Baron was planning the same for the United States. Murder and lust would reign rampant in the streets of every city in the land. Hundreds of thousands of men and women would die. Industry would stagnate; the wealth of the nation would be destroyed overnight—all to serve the selfish ends of the Scarlet Baron.

Kaleidoscopically, these thoughts raced through Jimmy Christopher's brain, as his fingers fumbled swiftly in the breast pocket of his coat. Diane, pressing close against him, shouted in his ear above the tumult:

"Jimmy! What'll we do? This mustn't go on. How can we stop it?"

"I'll stop it!" Jimmy told her grimly. He brought from his pocket an object that resembled a mechanical pencil, except that it was longer, and thicker. At one end of it was a red pin.

Diane's eyes widened when she saw it, for she recognized the thing. She had seen Jimmy Christopher use one of those pencil-like objects once before, knew it to contain a high explosive which Jimmy Christopher had perfected in his own laboratory. Fifty times more powerful than trinitrotoluene, there was enough of the substance in that container to destroy the entire building in which they now stood.

She gasped: "You—you're going to—?"

Jimmy nodded at the unspoken question in her eyes. "It's the only way, Diane. The whole country is in peril. If a thousand people die here tonight, what does it matter against the safety of a hundred million? You and I, Di, will go with them—and let us hope we will take the Scarlet Baron with us!"

Diane closed her eyes for a moment, clung tightly to his arm. "If—if you m-must, Jimmy!"

He gazed down at her tenderly, amid the wild tumult and the mad shouting, holding the pencil-bomb in the palm of his hand.

"Diane, dearest!" he said huskily. "In all the time that we've worked together, I've dreaded a moment like this. I've dreaded the thought that some time I would have to do a desperate thing like this, and destroy you, as well as myself. Diane, I wish you had never known me!" His mouth was a thin, grim line, and the muscles of his jaw were bunched tight. His eyes were bleak, filled with misery.

But Diane Elliot smiled bravely up at him, with eyes which were slightly misty. She whispered: "Jimmy, it's been worth it. I would not have it otherwise. I—I would rather die with you, than live without you."

There was a flash of admiration in Jimmy Christopher's eyes. He bent swiftly, brushed her lips with his. "Good-bye, Diane," he whispered.

Then he straightened, pulled the pin from the bomb, and hurled it toward the stage!

CHAPTER 6
THE MILLION-DOLLAR
REWARD

SEVEN BLOCKS from the Hippodrome, directly east on Forty-second Street, was the club-house and pier of the Metropolitan Flying Club. Behind the club building, a trim seaplane floated on its pontoons in the East River, moored to the short pier which jutted from the rear entrance of the house. Several dark-visaged men in dungarees were working on the ship, loading her with gasoline, testing the wings and the struts.

It would have been impossible for a casual visitor to have blundered into the club-house, for its door was made of massive oak, and the entire structure seemed to exude an atmosphere of expensive exclusiveness. If such a visitor had had the temerity to raise the ornate brass knocker that adorned the door, and to rap with it, a small aperture would have opened, and a baleful eye would have glared out, ordered him gruffly away.

However, if this visitor should have been able, in some miraculous way, to secure admittance, he would have been surprised at the interior of the exclusive-looking club. For the ground-floor rooms were piled high with weapons: machine-guns, automatics, Mills bombs, gas masks. A dozen men sat about in these rooms, in attitudes of tense expectancy. And the faces of those men would have given a distinct shock to the bold visitor, if he happened to be at all familiar with the pictures of the public enemies listed in the rogues' galleries of the country's police departments.

On the upper floor, a man sat in a dimly lit room, whose window faced east toward the river and the seaplane outside. His features were in shadow, blurred, indistinct. On the broad desk before him sat a number of instruments, including a microphone, a pair of headphones, and an annunciator box of the latest type.

The man was talking into the microphone. His voice was strong, imperious. His words were ringing, clear. They were the words that were at that moment being heard in the great auditorium of the Hippodrome. This man was the Scarlet Baron.

He was saying: "You shall share in the wealth that has been

accumulated through your misery. All right! Distribute the arms!"

He ceased speaking, and pushed the microphone away from him, touched a button on the desk. At once the door opened, and a thin, pinched-faced man in a peaked cap entered, stood respectfully before him.

"Franz!" the Scarlet Baron boomed. "Everything is ready? In five minutes, they will be ready to march from the Hippodrome. They will move downtown to the City Hall. In the meantime, you will take the men downstairs in the two armored cars, and cover their flanks. If any interference is offered by the police, you know what to do."

Franz nodded. "All set, boss. What about the seaplane?"

The Baron shrugged. "It looks as if I won't need it. I thought that maybe after that little fracas at the *Walnut Grove*, I might have to make a quick getaway. But I guess we've taken care of our friend, Operator 5. He's on the way to the precinct house now, and when he gets there that'll be the end of him. There won't be any more danger. Nothing can stop us!"

He reached forward, clicked on the annunciator box. "Let's hear what's going on at the Hippodrome."

While Franz waited, there came to them through the annunciator the confused murmur of voices from the big auditorium. The Baron chuckled. "The guns are being handed out. All those saps will storm the City Hall, and take over the city for us. Then we'll take it away from them. They will have used up all the ammunition we are issuing now, and it'll be easy for our men to disperse them. Their guns will be no good to them without bullets—"

HE STOPPED, aghast, as a thunderous sound filled the small room, emanating from the annunciator box. The dreadful explosion from the Hippodrome cracked against their eardrums, left the Baron and Franz speechless with consternation.

Franz took a swift step forward. "What's happened there, boss? God! That sounded like the end of the world!"

Suddenly the box became silent. No more sound issued from it. The Baron jiggled the key up and down desperately, but he could hear nothing. The instrument was dead.

Frantically he picked up the telephone, dialed a number. I'll call Lieber, who'd posted across the street in that small office we rented last week," he explained to Franz. "He'll know what's happened." He waited a moment, then barked into the phone: "Lieber! What's happening over there? What was that explosion—"

He stopped, listened to the high-pitched, frightened voice of Lieber. Slowly the knuckles that held the receiver whitened. "All right," the Baron said finally, huskily. "You can close up. I'm leaving New York at once. I'll communicate with you in the usual way in a few days."

When he hung up, the Baron said to Franz in a flat voice: "Somebody threw a bomb of some sort in the Hippodrome, just when they were giving out the guns. That crowd in there was stirred up to a white-hot heat, and everything would have gone off fine if it hadn't been for the bomb. Now, all our build-up in New York is shot to pieces. The Hippodrome is down in ruins, and about a hundred of the prize saps have been killed; also, forty or fifty of my own boys that were planted there to egg them on. The only thing that saved the others from being killed was the fact that the bomb was thrown at the stage, and caught in one of the drapes."

Franz stammered: "My God, boss, who could of thrown a bomb in there? It took pretty quick thinking to act that fast If it was a G-Man, how'd he get in there—?"

"It wasn't a G-Man," the Baron murmured softly. "I think I know who."

"You mean—Operator 5?"

"It sounds like something Operator 5 would do. I can't understand it, because Paulson said he was on his way to the precinct house. I—"

Suddenly he snapped his fingers, picked up the phone once more, dialed another number. "Kleed!" he rapped. "Did you take care of that business at the precinct house? Did Operator 5 get there?"

The voice at the other end was loud enough for Franz to hear. "No, boss, he didn't. That guy Hobson, the chief of G-Men, arrived alone. He must of dropped off Operator 5 some place on the way. Hobson went in to talk to Sweeney, so I figured we better give them the works anyway, even though Operator 5 wasn't there. We flooded the station house with gas, like you ordered. There ain't a rat left alive in there now."

The Scarlet Baron grunted into the phone, said: "All right, Kleed. It's not your fault that Operator 5 wasn't there. Sweeney won't talk, anyway. You get over to the Hippodrome. There's been an explosion of some sort; all my plans for tonight are squashed. Find out what happened to Cele Volney. If she's still alive, get her into hiding. I'm leaving the city for a week or so. When I return, I'll get in touch with you."

"Will you be safe, boss?" Kleed's voice asked anxiously. "After the business down at Greenwich Village, and this thing at the station house, the country'll be too hot to hold you."

The Baron chuckled. "They won't even know who I am yet, Kleed—any more than you do. And where I'm going, not even that damned Operator 5 will be able to find me!"

HE HUNG up, rested his chin in his cupped palms, with elbows on the desk. The motion brought his face into the light. And if anybody had been present there at the moment, besides Franz, that person would have gasped in unbelief; for the face of the Scarlet Baron was the face of a man who could not, by any stretch of the imagination, be here in New York at this time. It was the face of America's ex-Public Enemy Number One— Barney Broon! Barney Broon, who had been sentenced to life imprisonment, who at that moment was supposed to be locked snugly in a cell at Leander Prison, off the coast of Florida, was really far from his cell, in New York City!

Franz was grinning evilly. "You bet they won't know where to look for you, boss! But why scram? The riots are going over big in twenty cities. Even if it fizzles here in New York, we can still put it over—"

The Scarlet Baron shook his head. "You don't understand these things, Franz. Those riots will go on just the same, whether I'm here or not. And I can't afford to let them know yet, who I am. All these saps storming the treasury buildings and the city halls all over the country would swear by the Scarlet Baron—but would they follow Barney Broon? You know the answer. The Scarlet Baron is mysterious, appealing. There's no mystery about Barney Broon. Now they think they're fighting for a great cause—the Wealth-Sharing Movement. But if they knew Barney Broon was behind it, they wouldn't think it was so noble. Get the idea, Franz?"

Franz nodded eagerly. "I guess you got the brains, boss. So what do we do now?"

"We fly south, Franz. In the morning, Barney Broon will be in his cell at Leander again. And we'll let the G-Men comb the country for the Scarlet Baron. In the meantime, the riots will go on. Under cover of those riots, our boys will loot the treasury buildings and the banks, The Hippodrome explosion has put a crimp in the movement as far as New York goes. It'll take at least a week to build up another organization here. Then the Scarlet Baron will reappear."

He was about to rise from the desk when there came to them from downstairs the sounds of a sudden commotion. Men shouted, and scrambling feet beat against the stairs.

Franz swung toward the door, pulled it open. A breathless plug-ugly popped into the room, an automatic damped in his fist. "That damn kid!" the plug-ugly shouted wildly. "He's escaped! We had him downstairs in the cellar, all tied up. I just went down there, and he'd got his ropes off, an' was waitin' behind the door with a shovel! Look at the awful smack he gave me—" the speaker indicated a lump on the side of his head—"right on the bean. Then he slipped past me and went up the stairs to the main floor. He's hiding some place in the house!"

"Find him!" the Scarlet Baron raped. "I want that boy! He mustn't escape!"

"Well find him, boss," Franz vowed. "He can't get out of the house, that's a cinch. I'll put every man to turning the place inside out. We'll have him in ten minutes!"

The Scarlet Baron relaxed in his seat and Franz and the plug-ugly hurried out. The Baron turned his swivel chair around so that he could look out of the window. His eyes traveled over the trim lines of the seaplane at the pier, watched while the pilot climbed from the glass-enclosed cockpit, hoisted himself up on the port engine and examined the wings and struts.

Other men in white coveralls were working around the ship. Two of these were bent over the twin machine guns mounted atop the pilot's cubicle, between the engines. They were inserting the ends of long cartridge belts into the guns, running them under shatter-proof glass covering which protected them from rain and moisture. The two machine guns were set on a pivoting device controlled from the instrument-board. They were the newest development in aerial gun-mountings. In sheds on either side of the pier, lay two other seaplanes and men were working on these also, preparatory to rolling them out after the first had taken off.

THE BARON smiled grimly at the sight of the armament he controlled. As he watched, he saw a diminutive figure emerge from the rear entrance of the house, bearing a hamper of food. The small figure was clad in dungarees and a cloth-visored cap like the others, and strode with assurance toward the plane, mounted the gangplank, and descended into the passenger compartment. The Baron paid no further attention to that figure, assuming it to be one of his own men, engaged in provisioning the ship. Had he been able to catch a glimpse of the freckled face under that peaked cap, he would not have remained so cool. As it was, he swung from the window without suspicion as a knock sounded on the door.

He pressed a button on his desk, and the door opened to reveal the figure of Cele Volney!

The Baron sprang from his chair, exclaiming: "Cele! What happened at the Hippodrome? I thought you were there! How did you escape the explosion?"

The woman's carmine lips curved in a smile as she entered, closing the door behind her. "I was there all right," she explained. "And it was the luckiest accident that I'm here now to tell you about it!" Her cheeks were flushed with excitement, and she was breathing fast, her breasts rising and falling quickly.

The Baron came around the desk, held a chair for her. She dropped into it, glanced her thanks. "My dear Cele," he murmured, "I would have been the unhappiest man in the world if anything had happened to you. When I heard the explosion over the annunciator, my first thought was of you!"

"Yes," she said drily. "I see how much you think of me. You're making preparations to leave, without even trying to find out if I was still alive."

"You're wrong there, my dear. I've sent Kleed over to the Hippodrome, with instructions to locate you if he has to stay all night. But let's not waste time—his voice took on an edge of steel—"minutes are beginning to be precious. That damned kid we caught outside the *Walnut Grove* has broken loose, and he's somewhere in the house. When he's caught, we'll take him along with us into temporary retirement. I'll hold him till I find out the whereabouts of his friend, Operator 5!"

Cele Volney jerked her head up. "I can tell you where Operator 5 was. He caused the explosion at the Hippodrome. I saw him at the back of the house, with a girl. He was standing up in the crowd, talking to her, and when I spotted him, I got up and ran out backstage to get some of the boys to go after him. It was just as I looked back from the wings that I saw him hurl something. I guessed it was a bomb, and I ran for dear life. The explosion happened just as I got out the stage door!"

The Scarlet Baron's features contracted in rage. "I knew it was he!" He gripped Cele Volney's shoulder hard. "Do you think he died there?" he demanded tensely.

"I don't think so. The front part of the house is a mass of wreckage and debris and the whole roof has fallen in. But the people in the back, where Operator 5 and his girlfriend were standing, escaped because the balcony saved them. The balcony didn't collapse. A lot of people died in the stampede that followed, but I guess your—er—friend was smart enough to save himself!"

THE SCARLET BARON strode up and down the small room. Suddenly he turned and stood squarely before the woman. "Cele, we've got to get Operator 5 before he gets us! That man is a devil. He was supposed to be on his way to the station house to talk to Sweeney. I set a sweet trap for him there, but he didn't show up. Instead, he appears at the Hippodrome, wrecks the place just as I'm about to pull off the greatest *coup* of my campaign. With New York in the hands of the rioters, led by my men, I would have had control of the country! Now I've got to start over again. I'm going to concentrate every effort on finding him!"

He crashed one fist into the other. I'd pay a million dollars to the man who kills Operator 5 for me! I—"

He stopped as a knock sounded once more at the door. He strode to it, pulled it open. Franz stood there. "Sorry, boss," the little man

The explosion shook the building with the violence of a tropical hurricane!

86

whispered. "We can't find that boy. We've been over the whole house twice, but there's no trace of him. He couldn't have got out the front way, and the men working on the pier haven't seen him—"

"Search the house again!" the Baron barked. "He's somewhere. You keep on looking till you find him. I'm leaving now. I'll take Miss Volney, and six of the men. Let plane number two take off fifteen minutes later, with as many men as it can hold. You follow in number three, when you've found the boy. Leave instructions with Kleed and Lieber to get together as many survivors from the Hippodrome explosion as they can locate, and to hold them in readiness for orders at the various spots in the city. Lease a skeleton force in the house here. Now get out and keep on looking for that kid!"

"Yes, sir!" Franz stuttered. He hesitated. "That fellow, Paulson, is here. He's begging to see you. He says you told him he could come up. He needs a shot badly."

"To hell with him!" the Baron exclaimed. I don't need him anymore. Bring him in and give him the works; then throw him in the river!"

Franz started to leave, but the Baron suddenly stopped him. "Wait!" A sly look had come into his eyes. "I have a better idea. Send Paulson in here!"

Franz said: "Right, Boss!" and left.

Cele Volney looked at the Baron inquiringly. She was applying lipstick to her already-red lips. "You certainly change, your mind fast, don't you?" She stopped with the lipstick in the air, threw him a curious glance. "What are you cooking up for Paulson to do now?"

Broon laughed. "You don't think fast, Cele. That's your trouble. Didn't you just hear me say I'd pay a million dollars to have Operator 5 killed?"

Her eyes widened. "You—?"

"Exactly. Why pay a million, when I can have Paulson do it for nothing? He's crazy for a shot of the stuff in the branding needle. I won't give it to him. But I'll promise him a dose if he goes out and kills Operator 5. Who's in a better position than Paulson to do it? Paulson is a hero now. He's met Operator 5 already, will probably meet him again. And he'll do anything in the world for me!"

The Baron chuckled deep in his chest as he watched Cele Volney's fingers tighten involuntarily on the lipstick....

CHAPTER 7
MESSAGE FROM THE AIR

WHEN JIMMY CHRISTOPHER pulled the pin from the bomb and hurled it at the stage of the Hippodrome, he fully expected the next moment to be the last on this earth for Diane Elliot and himself.

So tense had he been, so stunned by the horror of the thing he was doing to all these innocent dupes—who were merely cat's-paws for the Scarlet Baron—that he did not notice Cele Volney leaving the stage. Even had he seen her depart, he would not have regretted it; for he felt somehow that the woman was not all bad.

But there was room in his mind for nothing except that he was deliberately consigning Diane, as well as hundreds of others in the auditorium, to a grisly death.

The explosion shook the old Hippodrome building with all the dreadful violence of a tropical hurricane. Flame sprang in sheets from the tinder-box stage; the whole front of the theater vanished in a holocaust of orange fire and roaring, deafening noise. Men's screams mingled with the thundering detonations, and a gaping hole appeared where the stage had been. Part of the Forty-third Street wall suddenly collapsed, bringing down with it a great section of the roof, which fell like a giant juggernaut, crushing the life from hundreds of men.

Those who had escaped that first blast, and the subsequent caving-in of the wall and the roof, began to flee in wild panic for the rear of the house. More of the roof fell, crushing them as they ran. Abruptly, the whole building was open to the night sky. Flames leaped high into the open void above. Men pinned under rafters screamed in agonizing pain, their shrieks drowned by the whirlwind of death about them.

Those in the rear were more fortunate than the others, for the falling roof was stopped by the tiers of balconies, giving them a breathing-space in which to scramble for safety. And that rout was wild, unthinking, panic-laden. Wildly clawing hands thrust neighbors aside ruthlessly, pushed them underfoot, and trampled them to death.

Men began pouring out from the exits, running, shrieking,

gasping for air. The heat within the crumbling building became unbearable as the flames mounted. And suddenly, to add to the horror, boxes of ammunition stored in the wings were reached by the greedy fire and began to crackle in a series of loud explosions.

The doorways were choked with terror-laden humanity struggling to reach the street. Outside, there was no one to give them assistance, to keep order. For the staccato firing which had been heard from the street had been the death-knell of the policemen stationed out there. Two men with sub-machine guns had slaughtered the bluecoats attempting to enter the Hippodrome at the first sounds of the battle within. Now they lay, dead, in the street, and their bodies were trampled by the fleeing exodus.

In the seething, cursing crowd that stormed out of the doomed building were Jimmy Christopher and Diane Elliot. Jimmy had dragged Diane out into the aisle as soon as he threw the bomb, had attempted to protect her as much as possible with his own body. As they were shoved along by the momentum of the crowd, his eyes grew bleak and gray. Never before had he found it necessary to sacrifice so many lives in the interests of his country. Each shriek that sounded from within—each agonized cry for help—was like an accusing finger pointed directly at him.

These people were, for the most part, innocent, moved to revolution by the silver-tongued oratory of the Wealth-Sharing speakers. Yet Operator 5 realized that they might have constituted a dreadful menace against the nation if they had gathered headway. Once in the streets, armed with the modern weapons which the Baron's men were distributing to them, they might have wreaked incalculable damage. Under cover of their ravages, the Scarlet Baron could have seized the city—seized New York, which was the heart of the nation. And there was no telling where that would have led to. Jimmy had heard enough from the Scarlet Baron himself to know that the disorders would continue until there was no longer a stable government in the land. Even now he was not at all sure that he had been able to upset the Baron's plans.

BUT HIS mind was torn away from these reflections by the press of people about him and Diane. Fire engines were arriving on the scene now, and the Hippodrome was disgorging hundreds of other panic-stricken men and women. Police cars, which had started for the scene even before the reports of the explosion, arrived, and the bluecoats began to get the crowd in check. Now there was no intention among the shivering, terror-stricken, hungry ones of marching on City Hall and demanding their share of the wealth of the nation. Those who had escaped the holocaust within wanted only one thing now—to get away as quickly as possible, to keep their share in the thing a secret. Figures began to slink away down Sixth Avenue and across Forty-Third Street. The crowd dwindled as rapidly as the firemen began to arrest the blaze.

Jimmy led Diane around the corner, saying nothing. She murmured:

"Jimmy! It—it was terrible! D-do you think the Scarlet Baron died in there?"

He shook his head grimly. "No, Diane. The Scarlet Baron wasn't there. I'm sure he was talking to that crowd through some sort of radio hook-up. He's too smart to have allowed himself to be caught. I'm afraid our work has just begun!"

Police kept arriving in ever-increasing numbers. The shooting outside the Hippodrome, just before the explosion, had brought them down on a general alarm. Now, a red-faced lieutenant from headquarters shouted orders, and the bluecoats established a cordon about the corner, with service revolvers openly in their hands. The sight of their comrades, lying riddled with machine-gun bullets, stirred them to bitterness, and they showed little consideration for the crowd. It became evident that no one would be allowed to depart. They were going to hold everybody there for questioning in headquarters.

Forty-Third Street, as well as Sixth Avenue, was now full of fire-fighting apparatus. Crash after crash resounded as the walls of the Hippodrome crumbled and caved in. Everybody who was ever going to escape from that flaming tomb was out now. The firemen were playing streams of water on the gutted building from a dozen nozzles. They stayed outside, for it would have been certain death to venture into that blazing hell.

Suddenly, while Jimmy and Diane watched from the middle of the street, the whole remaining structure buckled, crashing to the ground with a thunderous roar. Bricks and bits of glass hurtled down among the crowd. Flames shot upward in unbridled fury. The air about them became hot, dense with smoke and fire. Heat scorched the faces of those who watched.

Jimmy Christopher became aware that Diane was clinging to him, white-faced and trembling, and that his arm was tight around her. He groaned inwardly. "God forgive me, Diane," he whispered. "I've caused the death of all those people in there."

"You had to do it, Jimmy," Diane consoled him. "There was no other way. You destroyed them just as firemen demolish a row of houses to keep fire from spreading to the rest of a city. Their death was necessary; Jimmy—and you were ready to die with them!"

"I wish I could have, Diane!" he whispered. "As long as I live I'll never be able to rid myself of the picture of this funeral pyre of theirs; I'll never be able to stuff my ears against the sound of their dying shrieks!"

He turned a gray face away from the burning building, and his eyes narrowed at sight of a sedan which had pulled up across the street, at some distance from the police lines.

"Diane!" he exclaimed. "Take a look at the man in that car! Recognize him?"

She glanced quickly in the direction he had indicated, but shook her head dazedly. "I—I don't think so, Jimmy. I don't—think I'd recognize anybody—right now."

"It's Morton Kleed!" Jimmy told her urgently. "Remember him? Kleed was Barney Bison's right hand man. He was tried with Broon, and convicted, but he only got two years. He was released a short while ago. Diane! We've got to get away from here. I want to follow Kleed!"

EVEN AS he spoke, the sedan in which Morton Kleed sat began to move, backed into a driveway and made a complete turn in the street, heading in the opposite direction. Kleed was driving away. The police were heading all traffic back, away from the fire and the cordon.

Jimmy Christopher took his arm from around Diane, seized her wrist and started after the car. A burly policeman, with revolver in his hand, blocked his way roughly, shoving him back.

"Hey!" the bluecoat demanded. "Where do you think you're goin'? Nobody leaves here—in case you don't know it!"

Jimmy threw a hopeless glance at Diane. The sedan with Kleed in it was moving slowly down the street. It would have been useless to order the police to hold that car, apprehend Kleed. That was the last thing Jimmy Christopher wanted. If Kleed were connected with the Scarlet Baron, he would have shut up like a clam, given them no information. The thing to do was to trail the car, observe the man. If he were involved with the Baron, he might eventually lead them to his leader's retreat.

Jimmy Christopher said hastily to the cop: "I'm a Department of Justice Agent, officer. Here are my credentials." He produced the papers establishing his identity as George Wakely, of the Department of Justice. The cop scrutinized them doubtfully, while dozens of those in the crowd watched closely.

"Sorry, mister," the bluecoat shook his head "I got orders to let nobody through here unless I know them personally. The President himself couldn't get out of this cordon without bein' identified. If you want to wait while I call the lieutenant—"

Jimmy sighed. By the time the lieutenant came, that sedan would be gone.

Suddenly Diane spoke up. "Haven't I met you before, officer?

95

You ought to know me. I'm the reporter for the Amalgamated Press—"

The bluecoat grinned. "Why hello, Miss Elliot. Sure I remember you. You was the hostess at the breakfast the Amalgamated Press gave for the police academy when I was attendin' there last year. Sure I know you. Go right through!"

Diane smiled gratefully. "And this gentleman—?"

The cop shook his head. "Sorry, Miss Elliot. I couldn't let him through without the lieutenant's okay,"

Diane glanced at Operator 5. "I'll go, Jimmy," she said "I'll call you back at headquarters as soon as I get something." He nodded. "All right, Di, and good luck to you."

She pressed his hand. "And don't brood about this thing here, Jimmy. It—it had to be done. And it took a brave man to do it!

She forced a wan smile at the cop, and was gone. Jimmy watched her hurry down the street after the slowly moving sedan, which was already almost at the corner. Soon her trim figure was lost to sight….

AN HOUR later, Jimmy Christopher was pacing up and down in the office of United States Intelligence, which he had left earlier that night in the company of John Hobson. Z-7 sat at his desk, shuffling through a sheaf of flimsies, which he handed one by one to a portly, bald-headed man who sat opposite him. The portly man was the Secretary of War, the final source of authority, next to the President, over the Intelligence Service. Z-7, the operating chief of Intelligence, was responsible only to this man. And he was now making his report, while Jimmy Christopher listened impatiently.

"That's the last of them, sir—so far," said Z-7 as he handed the last sheet of paper to the Secretary. "That makes fifteen cities in which the riots are spreading. My men are powerless to cope with the thing. What forces the local authorities have been able to muster in each case have proved inadequate against the well-armed mobs. These are definitely not sporadic uprisings of discontented people. They are units of a well-planned movement. The meeting at the Hippodrome was an example. If Operator 5 hadn't stopped that, New York would be weltering in blood right now. We've got to take over from the local authorities, sir, and throw the whole strength of the regular army into the task of crushing this uprising!"

The Secretary of War frowned. "My God, man," he exclaimed. "Do you mean to sit there and tell me that we're up against something as big as that? This Scarlet Baron is nothing more than a big-scale criminal. If we have to declare a state of insurrection for a thing like this, what would we do if a *real* revolution broke out?"

Operator 5 stopped his pacing, faced the Secretary tensely. "You've got to understand, sir," he said urgently. "*This* is a real revolution. If it's not crushed tonight, it'll snow us under. The Scarlet Baron has deliberately crippled all the government agencies that might have opposed him. The Federal Bureau of Investigation is completely disrupted. With the massacre of the G-Men downtown, he's proved to his followers that he fears nothing. These mobs in the various cities don't know yet that their leader is really the Scarlet Baron. When he reveals himself, it'll be too late for them to back out. They'll have murdered and pillaged, and burnt their bridges behind them. They'll have to go along with him. His ambition is to make himself the ruler of the United States—I can assure you he will actually rule within a week unless you take drastic steps to crush these uprisings. You've got to throw well-armed, regular troops into the territories where these mobs are growing. You've got to treat them like revolutionists—and not like scattered mobs who can be dispersed by a stream of water from a hydrant, or by firing blank bullets over their heads!"

The Secretary of War shook his head stubbornly. "I am not yet convinced, Operator 5, that your theory is the correct one. It is true that the mob here in the Hippodrome might have proved highly dangerous had you not headed it off so courageously. Yet that further proves that the United States Army is not needed. One man was sufficient to cope with the problem here in New York; why should it require more in the other cities? Let us send agents into those cities. Let the governors of the various states concentrate the National Guard in the troubled areas. Let us focus every effort on the task of discovering who this Scarlet Baron really is. When we have identified him, we shall have little trouble in rounding him up, and that will be the end of the whole thing. Why, gentlemen—" he arose, and glared at them—"this country would make itself the laughing-stock of the world if we should take seriously an abortive thing like this. The governments of the world would laugh up their sleeves at a country which had to call out its regular army to battle a slimy criminal like this Scarlet Baron!"

JIMMY CHRISTOPHER faced the portly man, with

unbelief in his eyes. "You mean, sir, that you're not going to take official cognizance of this revolt?"

"Of course not!" the Secretary snapped. "I am going far enough in permitting Intelligence to spend its time on this, when there are so many international problems facing us. But since you are working on it, there should be no difficulty in discovering the identity of the Scarlet Baron. Turn your attention to that instead of trying to coax me into making a fool of the nation by calling out the regular army. Find out who the Scarlet Baron is—"

"I think, sir," Jimmy broke in quietly, "that I know who he is!"

Both Z-7 and the Secretary pressed forward eagerly. "You—know?"

"I think," Jimmy Christopher told them, "that the Scarlet Baron is—*Barney Broon!*"

Z-7's eyebrows drew together in a frown, while the Secretary burst into derisive laughter. "Barney Broon!" he repeated incredulously. "Why man, are you mad? Broon is in Leander Prison. You tell us that you talked to the Scarlet Baron in New York. The Scarlet Baron addressed the mob in the Hippodrome tonight. And yet you stand there with a straight face and inform us that the Scarlet Baron is Barney Broon!"

"I only say I *think* he is, sir. Broon may be out of Leander—"

The Secretary frowned impatiently. "We'll settle that right now!" He reached for the phone on Z-7's desk, rasped into the transmitter:

"Get me Warden Manlcy, at Leander Prison, in Florida. Quick!"

He hung up, glared at Jimmy. "We'll soon settle that point. Now maybe you can think up some more jokes while we're waiting!"

Z-7 sighed, addressed the Secretary quietly. "Operator 5 has been under a great strain, sir. You must remember that a thing like that affair at the Hippodrome tonight really entitles a man to rest. You cannot expect him to function smoothly immediately after such an ordeal." He turned to Operator 5. "Look, Jimmy, why don't you go home and get some sleep? You've done more than your share tonight—"

Jimmy Christopher took an impulsive step forward. Between himself and Z-7 there had grown a bond of deep affection, almost that of father and son. He knew that Z-7 sincerely felt he had been under too great a strain—had probably cracked temporarily, and need a rest. "You think I'm mad, Chief," he said. "But this whole business is mad. Would you have said, a month ago, that it was possible for such things to happen in the United States as have happened here tonight? Of course not. I'm waiting to hear from Diane, now. She followed a man who drove up to the Hippodrome right after the accident, and then drove away. That man, Chief, was Morton Kleed, who used to be Barney Broon's assistant. If Kleed was interested in this, I'll bet anything that Broon is also interested." He frowned worriedly, glanced at his wrist watch. "I should have heard from Diane by now. If anything's happened to her—"

He was interrupted by the ringing of the phone. The Secretary picked it up, barked: "Hello! Yes, Manley, I want to talk to you. I'm going to ask you a crazy question—is Barney Broon in Leander Prison at this minute, or isn't he?... Speak up, man, I can't hear you.... What? You say he is? Crazy question, eh? What makes me ask? There's a young man here that's advancing wild theories, and I thought I'd squelch him.... No, not a mad general; a mad Intelligence Agent.... You've heard of him—Operator 5—" the Secretary winked at Jimmy tolerantly, spoke into the phone —"a good man; but the best of them will go batty once in a while. All right, Manley, you can go back to sleep. Good-bye!"

He hung up with a triumphant look. "Well, young man? What's your next theory? Maybe—"

He was interrupted by a knock at the door. Two Intelligence Agents entered, their faces red from the cold of the street Jimmy Christopher knew them both. They were M-14 and S-2. S-2 glanced hesitantly at Jimmy, but addressed Z-7. "We went to investigate that clubhouse on the East River, sir, where the patrolman said he saw three seaplanes take off within a few minutes of each other. The place was deserted, and we searched it. In the cellar, we found this!"

He extended his hand, palm up. In there lay a small ring, at the sight of which Jimmy Christopher uttered a hoarse exclamation of dismay. He snatched it from S-2's hand, examined it closely. It was fashioned of white metal, with a white skull on a black background. In addition to the numeral "5" on the forehead of the skull, there was a secret symbol on the ring which identified it without doubt....

IT WAS the ring which Operator 5 had given to Tim Donovan, by which he could identify himself to any Intelligence

Agent. Agents all over the world had been advised of the ring—
of the fact that the boy who wore it was Operator 5's unofficial
assistant. The eyes of S-2 met those of Operator 5 in a sympa-
thetic glance. Both knew what the finding of that ring in the
cellar of the house meant.

Jimmy Christopher's shoulders sagged as he clutched the
ring tightly.

"Tell me all about it!" he demanded hoarsely.

"There's not much to tell, Operator 5," S-2 said soberly. "The
cop on the beat phoned in, and we went there, entered with him.
The front door was unlocked, and there was nobody in the place.
There were signs all around that it had been left hastily. Down in
the cellar, we found this ring. It was lying on the shovel, and the
shovel had bloodstains along one edge of it. I'm sorry, Operator
5, but I'm afraid that was Tim Donovan's blood!"

Jimmy Christopher turned away from S-2 to meet the
commiserating glance of Z-7. The Intelligence Chief was
perhaps the only one there who knew how close were the ties
between his ace operative and the freckle-faced boy.

Jimmy's mouth was a tight, thin line. He said huskily: "Chief,
I'm going over to that clubhouse. Maybe I can find some clue
that's been overlooked—something that'll help me to find
Tim—"

"Look here, Operator 5!" the Secretary of War broke in. "I'm
awfully sorry to hear about the boy. But we've got other things
to consider. Hundreds have died tonight, both here in New York,
and in other cities where riots have taken place. If the Scarlet

Baron is not identified and located in short order, thousands more may die. Your duty lies here, not searching for the boy—"

Jimmy Christopher's eyes blazed. "Then why don't you call out the troops? If you feel this is so important, why don't you treat it that way?"

"Because, my boy, we can't afford to admit to the world that we have such a serious internal upheaval. Europe is watching us like a hawk; so is the Orient. News dispatches telling of riots here and there will mean little. But the news that we have a revolution which necessitates the use of our regular army will make these other nations sit up and take notice. All they need is knowledge like that to unleash their war-dogs against our far-flung outposts. The Philippines, still safe in their new-found independence, would be gobbled up overnight if it were suspected that we had a revolution at home!"

The Secretary's manner had changed subtly. He became confidential, put an arm around Jimmy's shoulders. "My boy, it is more than mere obstinacy on my part when I refuse to use the regular army. Believe me, I appreciate the gravity of the situation. In twenty-four hours, these riots may spread into nationwide civil war. But until we are actually forced to, we must do nothing that will encourage the idea that our hands would be tied against foreign aggression. You should realize this as well as I do."

Jimmy bowed his head. "Perhaps you're right, sir. I—I'm sorry if I was rude—"

"That's all right, Operator 5. I understand how you feel. Tim Donovan was very close to you —" he stopped momentarily as he saw Jimmy wince at his use of the past tense, then went on hurriedly—"yet, only a few hours ago, you were willing to sacrifice your own life and that of a certain young lady, in order to save the city from being bathed in blood. You must now give up the thought of searching for Tim Donovan, and concentrate on finding the Scarlet Baron. I feel that you are the best man for the work. I shall rely on you. I am sure you will not fail the nation now, any more than you have in the past!"

JIMMY RECOGNIZED in the Secretary's tone and in his words, the subtle flattery which was calculated to inspire him to redoubled effort. It was the stock-in-trade of the clever statesman. Yet the Secretary was urging him to do what he himself felt he should do. Too often in the past had he disregarded personal safety and the safety of those he loved in the service of the nation. He would not weaken now.

He nodded bitterly. "All right, sir. I'll do whatever you say. But perhaps by seeking Tim I may find the Scarlet Baron. From

CELE VOLNEY

THE SCARLET BARON

PAULSON

what S-2 reports, the clubhouse was the headquarters of the Baron—"

He was interrupted by a knock at the door, followed by the entry of an agent in shirtsleeves from the outer office. The agent glanced at Z-7, said: "We're picking up a message on the wireless set, sir. It's in code, but the sender seems to be giving Operator 5's code letters. I thought maybe—"

Jimmy Christopher did not give him a chance to finish. His eyes had suddenly begun to sparkle. Only one person could be sending a message in code, and using his code letters; and that person was Tim Donovan!

Months ago, Jimmy Christopher had devised a code which was a variation of the Morse System, and which he had taught to Tim for special use in communicating between the two. An expert wireless operator himself, he had taught the boy how to send and receive, and Tim had gone on from there, using his natural ingenuity to master the art of the clicking key. And here was a message from him, coming over the air!

Jimmy pushed the agent aside, rushed out into the telegraph room. The operator hastily got up from his chair before the instrument, making room for Jimmy, who took the key. Over it was coining the repetition of six dashes in a row, which Jimmy had assumed as his code signal. This he had based on the International instead of the Morse code. In the Morse, the letter "O" would ordinarily be represented by *dot, dot;* whereas the International used three dashes. Since the numeral 5 in the American code was represented by three dashes, the signal for 0-5 became six dashes, which combination of the two systems automatically labeled a message as coming from Tim.

Feverishly Jimmy Christopher seized the key, sent out into the ether the signal for Tim: "T.D.! T.D.!"

While the Secretary of War and Z-7, who had followed him out, watched him eagerly, Jimmy shot out into the ether:

"I'm getting you, Tim. Ready to receive!"

There flashed back, in their special stenographic code: "Thank God, Jimmy! I thought you were killed in the Hippodrome explosion. Are you okay?"

"I'm okay," Jimmy clicked back impatiently. "Where are you? What happened?"

"I don't know where I am, Jimmy, except that I'm in a seaplane somewhere over Delaware. Raid the clubhouse of the Metro-politan Flying Club. It's the headquarters of the Scarlet Baron, It's probably too late—"

Jimmy broke into the message to click: "Flying Club already raided. Nothing found but your ring. How did you get in seaplane?"

"I was prisoner in Clubhouse. Put on steward's suit, and carried hamper of food into seaplane, stowed away on it. Scarlet Baron on board with Cele Volney. Sneaked into wireless room while operator is eating. Don't know where we're bound for, but plane is heading south. Will try to keep in touch with you...."

Suddenly the message trailed off in a series of meaningless dots. Then the instrument became silent.

Jimmy raised haggard eyes to Z-7 and the Secretary of War.

"It was Tim, all right! He's on a plane bound south, but he

doesn't know the destination. The Scarlet Baron is on board. Something must have happened, because his message was cut off in the middle. I'm afraid he's been caught!"

CHAPTER 8
BATTLE ON THE PARAPET

THE SECRETARY of War bent forward eagerly. "See if you can pick him up again, Operator 5! Try, man! Try to get him again! Didn't he say who the Scarlet Baron was?"

Jimmy shook his head. "Either he doesn't know, or he didn't get a chance to finish. Something's happened on that plane, or he'd still be on the air."

Hopelessly his fingers moved to click out the signal but there was no response.

He arose slowly, yielded the chair to the regular operator. "Watch that instrument every minute!" he ordered tensely. He swung around, faced the Secretary of War. "Mr. Secretary, we've got to stop that plane. If you please, I'd like to have you order up every army ship available in the territory. Tim said they were somewhere over Delaware, heading south. The skies must be fine-combed. Every seaplane must be stopped, grounded. Throw a patrol of pursuit planes across Chesapeake Bay and up the Potomac, then around in a circle from Washington to Philadelphia. We've got to block in the territory through which that seaplane is flying, so that not even a fly can pass through. We'll force the Scarlet Baron back into New York!"

The Secretary of War nodded eagerly. "That's the ticket,

Operator 5. I'll have two hundred planes in the air inside of fifteen minutes!"

He snatched up the nearest phone, dialed a number with shaking fingers. "If we catch the Scarlet Baron through Tim Donovan's efforts, by gad, I'll see to it that that boy gets a Congressional Medal!" He got his number, began to bark orders into the phone.

Jimmy Christopher's eyes were somber. He saw Z-7 gazing at him, and knew that the chief was aware of his thoughts. A few minutes ago, before the wireless message came in, he had thought Tim Donovan either dead or a captive. The news that Tim was alive and kicking had come startlingly, dramatically. But there was little cause for rejoicing. The abrupt ending of the message could only mean that the boy had been caught. And even if he had not, Jimmy had just sentenced Tim Donovan to death. If any of those pursuit planes which the Secretary of War was sending up in droves, should sight the amphibian, Jimmy had no doubt that the Scarlet Baron would not descend without an attempt to flee—with the result that he would be literally blasted out of the air by the army fliers. And Tim would die in the crash.

Bitterly, Jimmy Christopher reflected that it seemed always to be his fate to have to thrust his loved ones into the jaws of death.

He forced himself to consider the matter at hand. M-14 and S-2 had followed them from the private office and Jimmy called them over. "What was the layout of the Metropolitan Flying Club?" he asked, while the Secretary of War was still drumming orders into the phone.

"The ground floor must have been a sort of barracks. There were cots, and tables. Magazines and cards were scattered around, as if the men in there had left in a hurry. Upstairs, there is a room which was evidently used by the boss. It has a microphone which is connected to a miniature radio sending-station on the roof. There's also an annunciator, connected outside the building. We left some men there to trace it—"

"How about fingerprints?"

"We got about a dozen different prints, in that room alone, and rushed them down to police headquarters. There should be a report on them—"

HE WAS interrupted by Z-7, who was fingering through a sheaf of dispatches that had just been handed him. "Good God!" exclaimed the Chief. "The Scarlet Baron may be checked in New York, but he has things his own way everywhere else! Look at these!" He thrust the flimsies into Jimmy's hand as he read them. They were from Richmond, Charleston, Jacksonville, and half a dozen other cities in the south. The one from Richmond was typical of the others:

MW…NY… RIOTS OUT OF HAND HERE… MOB TOO POWERFUL FOR LOCAL FORCES… NATIONAL GUARD DRIVEN BACK BY OVER- WHELMING FORCES… MANY HAVE JOINED RIOT- ERS… MOB IN POSSESSION OF STATE CAPITOL… GOVERNOR KILLED… WHOLE STATE OF VIRGINIA CRIPPLED… CITIZENS BEING SHOT DOWN IN STREETS… FOR GOD'S SAKE GET SOMETHING

110

DONE… THIS IS REVOLUTION… R-VA….

Rapidly, Jimmy Christopher went through the others. The riots which were now taking place in the southern cities were, it seemed, even more serious than those reported earlier in the evening. Those had apparently been more a test of strength than anything else. These in the South seemed to be a determined, desperate effort to seize the reins of government in various state capitals. They were uniformly successful….

The Secretary of War had finished his telephoning, and Jimmy silently handed him the flash reports. The portly secretary's face went a sickly white as he perused them.

"This is dreadful!" he murmured. "See how they concentrate in the heart of each state—Richmond; Charleston; Jacksonville; New Orleans! They are effectively paralyzing resistance in each state—"

"It's the same system," Jimmy told him, "that most fascist revolutions use. They seize control of the governmental agencies in the local provinces. Mussolini acquired power that way, then marched on Rome. If these people march on Washington—"

"We've got to stop them!" the Secretary thundered. "I'll phone the President for authority to use the regular army. You were right—"

"I'm afraid it's too late now, sir," Jimmy said drily. "Where would you march first? This movement covers more than twenty states already. The regular army is pitifully small. You'd have to spread it out so thin that it would be ineffective. The time to crush this thing was when it was confined to two or three spots."

He glanced at a teletype operator who was hurrying toward

111

them with another message. The Secretary snatched it from the man's hands, read it hastily, with Jimmy Christopher and Z-7 looking over his shoulder. It was from Richmond:

MW... NY... RIOTERS IN COMPLETE—CONTROL... THEIR LOCAL LEADER IS ROUNDING UP ALL MEMBERS OF THE VIRGINIA STATE LEGISLATURE... WILL COMPEL THEM TO ENACT LAWS MAKING THEIR SEIZURE OF GOVERNMENT LEGAL... ARSENALS AND AIRPORTS IN THEIR HANDS... MEN POURING IN FROM ALL PARTS TO JOIN... ARE RECEIVING ARMS... PREPARATIONS BEING MADE TO MARCH ON WASHINGTON... WHY DON'T YOU REPLY TO PREVIOUS MESSAGES... WHAT ARE WE TO DO... R-VA....

Z-7 laughed mirthlessly. "They want a reply! What reply can I give them? Tomorrow we'll be swearing allegiance to the Scarlet Baron—or be given doses of castor oil!"

"But my God, man," the Secretary exclaimed, "who is the Scarlet Baron? Why does he keep in the background? If he's really behind all this, why doesn't he declare himself, and take charge of all these operations? How can we fight him when we don't know who he is? We've got to find that out! We've got to capture him. Then this whole revolt will collapse. Maybe the planes I ordered up will stop him!"

He glanced at his watch. "In a few minutes we should hear from the air patrols. He can't get through the net I'm spreading!"

JUST THEN, Z-7 looking across the busy room, nudged

Jimmy Christopher, nodding toward the door. "Here comes Paulson. He looks all in. Poor fellow, he never got over the massacre of his friends down at Greenwich Village."

Sigmoid Paulson had entered, and stood near the door for a moment, as if reluctant to go further. His shoulders were sagging, and his face was pasty, with beads of sweat on his forehead. His mouth showed a slight twitch, and in his eyes there was a tight, desperate look.

He saw Jimmy Christopher standing near the telegraph instrument, hesitated a moment, then hurried over. Z-7 smiled at him reassuringly, asked: "How goes it, Paulson? Have you got your men lined up?"

But Paulson merely mumbled an answer. His eyes were on Jimmy Christopher. "Can I see you alone for a few minutes, Operator 5?" he asked.

Jimmy gave him a puzzled glance. "Why, sure!" He walked a few steps away with the other, and Paulson whispered: "I want you to come up on the roof with me, Operator 5. There's something I want to show you; and no one else must see it. Please say nothing to these others. Just tell them that you will be back in a few minutes. I can't explain now."

Jimmy frowned. "These men here are all trusted agents, Paulson, if that's what's troubling you—"

"No, no. You must do as I ask, Operator 5. For God's sake, don't ask any more questions. Come quickly!"

Jimmy hesitated a second, then shrugged. He turned, said to Z-7: "Will you excuse me? I'll be right back." Then he followed Paulson out into the corridor, past the two agents stationed in

Jimmy raised his arm to ward off Paulson's murderous attack!

the small foyer, whose duty it was to keep out all but those who had business there. Paulson said nothing as they waited for the rising elevator, but Jimmy, studying him out of the corner of his eye, noted that something was quite evidently wrong with him. He seemed to be laboring under the stress of some great agitation.

Jimmy entertained no suspicion of Paulson. He said:

"What's this you want to show me on the roof? Must be pretty awful, from the way you're acting."

"It's something I want you to see from the roof. Wait till we get up there."

"Don't tell me you want to show me a sunrise!" Jimmy jibed. He was trying to raise the man's spirits, but Paulson seemed to be beyond any kind of humor. He merely looked at the floor morosely until the elevator arrived. They got off at the top floor, ascended the staircase to the roof.

This office of Intelligence, known as MW-NY, was at this time located on the nineteenth floor of the thirty-two story Fleer Building on Lexington Avenue near Thirty-Fifth Street.*

* AUTHOR's NOTE: The records in MW-NY are voluminous, since they dupli-cate the files of WDC-13, the permanent Intelligence Office in Washing-ton. In order to reduce to a minimum the danger of discovery, MW-NY as well as other offices, are moved frequently, lock, stock and barrel. Generally they masquerade under some innocent business name which appears on the door, and they are located in the most unlikely spots. There was a period when MW-NY was the Glenville Fish Market, with offices underneath a smelly, noisome store in which fish was sold at ridiculously low prices so as to justify the number of men who visited it. In the Fleer Building, at this time,

A few blocks north was the building in which the Department of Justice had its New York headquarters, and from which Paulson had supposedly come.

The Fleer Building was surrounded by other structures, many of them much taller. But there was a good view to be had from the roof of the East River and of Long Island.

PAULSON STRODE across the sanded roof to the parapet, and leaned far over, gazing toward the river. Jimmy watched him, looking out into the night in the same direction, but seeing nothing to warrant attention. To the north, and slightly west, a plume of smoke drifted upward. Jimmy shuddered. He knew that that drifting smoke indicated the spot where the Hippodrome had stood only a few hours before, and where hundreds had perished. Though he had saved New York from horrid bloodshed by his swift action in hurling the bomb, he still could not remove from his mind's eye the picture of the hundreds of men who had perished there. He felt that he would never rid himself of that nightmare. Had he known that he was going to survive the throwing of that bomb, he might never have done it. It was only the thought that he was visiting the same destruction upon himself that had given him the courage to hurl it.

Even now, he thought that he would like to die as a sort of atonement to the hundreds of victims of that holocaust. He

the name on the door was: "Greyhound Advertising Agency." It occupied the entire 19th floor, and had one office for legitimate advertising clients, of whom there were quite a few, and another entrance for the agents, who posed as advertising canvassers for the firm.

turned his gaze away from the north, and leaned over, trying to find what Paulson was supposed to be looking for.

Suddenly Paulson, peering downward, and leaning far over the parapet, pointed with an appearance of great excitement at something almost directly below. "There it is, Operator 5!" he exclaimed, "Take a look at that, and tell me what you think of it!"

He straightened up, his eyes bright, waited for Jimmy to bend over.

Jimmy Christopher, still puzzled, leaned over, gazed down in the direction in which the other had pointed. He saw nothing worthy of attention. The building opposite was dark, and the street, far below, deserted. Behind him, Paulson's foot scraped on the flooring. He had drawn his revolver. Clubbed in his fist, the gun made a vicious, silent weapon, capable of smashing a man's skull if swung with sufficient force.

Paulson raised the gun overhead, his body taut, his eyes gleaming madly in the darkness.

Though Jimmy Christopher had not suspected the man, his senses were always keyed up to the alert. Things that might have made no impression on the average man registered with him almost subconsciously. Now, as he leaned over that parapet, a single thing impressed itself on him: Any man, pointing something out to another, would lean over with him, and indicate the object he wished noted. Paulson, however, had not done so. The scrape of Paulson's foot indicated that he was stepping backward.

In that instant, the sixth sense which had so often preserved Operator 5's life in ticklish spots, whispered to him urgently of danger. He sensed that Paulson was now directly behind him, when he should have been alongside him according to all the laws of human behavior. And Jimmy Christopher straightened, moving lithely to one side.

THE VICIOUS blow which Paulson had aimed at the back of Operator 5's head whizzed against Jimmy's ear, scraping it painfully, landed on his right shoulder with a numbing impact to send twinges of fire down the length of his arm. His ear burned as if a searing iron had been placed against it. He heard Paulson's grunt of frustrated rage, and swung around, raising his left arm just in time to parry a second swiping blow of the murderous clubbed gun. The bone handle of the revolver struck his raised forearm, paralyzing it. His arm was smashed downward, but the force of the blow was broken. It struck his forehead, inflicting a long gash over the left eye.

Blood from the gash blinded Jimmy as he stepped backward quickly, helpless before the mad desperation in Paulson's face. Both his arms hung limp at his sides. No word was spoken between the two men. Jimmy knew that it would be of no help to him to cry out, for his shouts would be unheard up there.

He shook his head to clear the blood from his eyes, while hot pains seared his shoulder and right arm—while tingling numbness deadened his left.

Paulson was close to him, hot breath in his face, revolver raised again for the finishing blow. His lips were drawn back from his teeth in an animal snarl, and there was no mercy in his eyes.

Jimmy moved, in spite of his handicap, with split-second efficiency. He bent at the knees, and swayed to one side, just as

Paulson's arm swept down upon him. The arching metal once more missed his head, scraped against his helpless right arm; and as Paulson's swing carried him slightly forward, Jimmy lunged forward, head low, his legs uncoiling like two high-tension springs suddenly released.

The top of Jimmy Christopher's head caught Paulson in the stomach, sent him backward with a grunt of forcibly expelled breath. He went toppling against the parapet, and Jimmy's momentum sent him after the treacherous agent. Jimmy twisted his body so that his left shoulder smacked against Paulson's midriff.

Paulson had not yet recovered his breath, and the second blow at his diaphragm left him doubled over, gasping for air and twisting like an epileptic.

Jimmy had dropped to the flooring, and now he pushed himself to his feet without the aid of his hands. Paulson's face was gray and drawn, and he was moaning in agony. He still clutched the revolver.

Jimmy Christopher's eyes were bleak and cold. The pain in his shoulder and right arm was almost unbearable, though he was gradually recovering the use of his left He said curtly: "Drop the gun, Paulson!"

The other let go of the weapon, and it clattered to the floor. He was squirming in agony, though beginning to draw in great gasps of air.

Jimmy could not reach his own gun, which was in the holster under his left armpit. To raise his right arm was impossible. Even to move it ever so slightly caused exquisite torture. The blow on the shoulder must have smashed some of the small bones there. To maneuver the gun out of the holster with his left arm was difficult, with the numbness still causing it to tingle down its entire length. He therefore bent to pick up Paulson's revolver.

And Paulson's foot came up like lightning in a smashing kick to the side of Jimmy's head. The toe of the agent's shoe thudded against Jimmy Christopher's temple with a dull thud, and Operator 5 was hurled backward to land on the roof, face up. A giant black hand seemed to be gripping his brain, digging thick hard fingers into it and twisting mercilessly. Blackness engulfed his sight....

He fought against unconsciousness, exerting every ounce of his will-power to repel the wave of helplessness that surged over him. The cruel agony in his head increased. Something seemed to be pushing him into oblivion. As if in a dream he felt himself being lifted bodily, raised to the parapet. Subconsciously, he heard Paulson grunt with the effort of lifting him. He was hanging over the parapet now, head foremost above the street, thirty-two floors below. And he felt Paulson's hands upon him, pushing him relentlessly....

CHAPTER 9
TRAIL OF THE BARON

TO MOST men, the thought of a thirty-two story plunge to an asphalt pavement below is a numbing prospect which paralyzes the nerves in a wave of icy panic. Upon Jimmy Christopher, it acted like a pail of cold water dashed in the face of a punch-drunk boxer. It drove the blackness from his brain, and spurred the reflexes of his splendidly muscled body to desperate effort.

It was not that Operator 5 feared death in itself. Too often had death jogged at his elbow. The grim specter was no stranger to him. He played a game with death, and like every true sportsman, he tried hard to win. But the stakes in this game were more than life itself now.

Jimmy Christopher's brain was still in a swimming fog of pain, he yet realized his peril. The parapet was perhaps six inches wide. The cold masonry lay against his stomach, and Paulson, behind, was pushing at him. It needed only a slight shove to send him over into the canyon yawning for him. Acting more from instinct than from reasoned calculation, he did a thing that no other man would have had the courage to do. He kicked upward with his legs, virtually sending his body hurtling out into space. Then, almost in the same motion, his legs came together, met in a scissors hold about Paulson's throat.

There was little to lose by the maneuver; for in another instant, by remaining quiescent, his assailant would have shoved him over the side. Had Jimmy's subconscious action missed by only an inch, he would have gone over a split-second before Paulson's efforts could have accomplished the same thing. As it was, his body's forward motion was cut short sharply by the scissors hold.

Hanging that way, with his head down, he put every fiber of his strength into tightening that scissors hold.

Behind him, Paulson grunted, beat frantically against Jimmy's legs and thighs, but to no avail. The inexorable grip tightened.

Paulson dug his fingers into Jimmy's legs, trying to pinch, to scratch. But Operator 5's leg muscles, bulging with the strain of the grip, afforded only a hard steel-like surface. Slowly, Jimmy Christopher's body moved forward over the parapet, dragging Paulson with him.

And the treacherous agent, suddenly giving way to panic as he understood that his victim was bent on dragging him over too, began to push away from the parapet with both hands. His throat clamped in the vise-like grip of those two hard-muscled legs, he could barely grunt his fear. He pushed madly, frantically, and gradually Jimmy's body began to move backward toward safety.

Jimmy's left hand had lost most of its numbness by now, and he reached up, gripped the top of the parapet, and heaved himself upward. In a moment he was lying atop the masonry, his grip on Paulson's throat relaxed.

Paulson dodged out of the scissors hold, panting, red-faced. But before he could leap in again, Jimmy had swung lithely back on to the roofing, side-stepped the agent's mad rush. He brought up his left fist in a short smash to the other's jaw which sent Paulson dropped in a heap at his feet.

Jimmy drew in a deep breath, and stood spread-legged there on the roof, while, his brain swam dizzily. Paulson lay still....

THE DOOR from the elevator bank burst open, and Z-7 came rushing out. The Intelligence chief stopped short as he saw the tableau, exclaimed: "Jimmy! I came up to see what was keeping you so long. What's been happening here?"

Operator 5 laughed hollowly. "Nothing much, chief. Paulson and I have just been rough-housing each other a little!"

Z-7 came closer, stared down at the unconscious agent Jimmy told him swiftly what had happened. Z-7 looked almost incredulous. "Good God, Jimmy!" he said huskily. "Why would he want to kill you?"

For answer, Jimmy bent, tore open Paulson's coat and shirt. There, under the left armpit, was the scarlet letter "B" branded into the agent's flesh.

Z-7 gasped. "The Scarlet Baron's man! But Paulson! One of the most trusted agents—how could he have come under the Baron's influence?"

"Somehow," Jimmy hazarded, "they must have got him to agree to be branded. Maybe he contacted them, the way I did. I wouldn't let them brand me, but he must have agreed. And once he was branded, he was really the Baron's man. The hypodermic needle inserted a dose of some powerful habit-forming drug, and he had to have more of it or go insane. He would do anything the Baron ordered." Jimmy took from his pocket the small electric machine he had picked up at the *Walnut Grove*, and looked at it speculatively.

"I haven't had a chance to analyze the contents of this thing yet. But whatever it contains, it's made a traitor of Paulson!"

Between them, they carried the unconscious man into the elevator, and down to the nineteenth floor. The elevator operator asked no questions. He had learned that it was better to maintain a discreet silence about the things done by the men from that floor.

Back in the office, they left Paulson in a room with a guard, and went back to Z-7's private office, where they found the Secretary of War pacing up and down like a caged wild-cat. He waved a flimsy before them, fairly thrust it into Jimmy Christopher's hand.

"Look at that! My God, that Scarlet Baron is as slippery as an eel!"

Jimmy read the sheet, showed it to Z-7. It was from the Anacostia Naval Station.

> Lieutenants Glendon and Marsh sighted seaplane flying south and attempted to stop it. Were shot down by two other seaplanes following the first. All three ships have slipped through our patrols. Regret this failure.

It was signed by the commander of the station.

The Secretary of War said bitterly: "He regrets this failure! My God, they let that crook slip through, let him shoot down two planes, and all they can say is: 'Regret this failure!' Is there nobody who can do something? Why didn't that kid tell you who this Scarlet Baron was? Here he is, flying south. We know he's in that seaplane, and we can't even stop him!"

He went on, talking incoherently, irascibly, while Z-7 fidgeted.

Jimmy Christopher turned away from the secretary as one of the men in the office tapped him on the shoulder.

"There's a chap outside, Operator 5, that wants to talk to you. Won't give any name, but says he has a message from a young lady friend of yours. Shall I send him in?"

Jimmy frowned. Suddenly an icy chill of apprehension seized

him. He remembered that he hadn't heard from Diane since she had gone after Kleed. He turned abruptly, took the agent by the arm. "I'll go out and talk to him!"

HE WENT into the foyer, and the agent indicated a small, wizened little man who was sitting on the bench, holding his black felt hat in his lap, and twisting it nervously. The man was about forty, and entirely bald. There was nothing prepossessing about him except for his fingers, which were long and slender, and might have belonged to an artist, a musician—or a pickpocket! He blinked fearfully at Jimmy Christopher, out of watery eyes.

"Are you Operator 5?" he asked in a quavering voice.

Jimmy eyed him suspiciously. This man, innocent appearing as he was, might be another emissary of the Scarlet Baron's. He was watchful as he replied: "I am Operator 5. Quick, man! What's your message?"

The little fellow rose and faced Jimmy. "I got to be sure you're the right man. You got something to identify you?"

Jimmy seized him fiercely by the lapels of his coat, bunching them together in his fist. "I tell you I'm Operator 5. Talk fast. What's your message—and who is it from?"

The little man's jaw sagged open in fear. "Sa-ay! What's the big idea? I only asked you for proof. The lady said I was to be sure I give the message to Operator 5, and to no one else. I'm only following instructions!"

Jimmy sighed, let him go, and took from his pocket a metal card-case which he snapped open with his thumb. Within it was a document, under a sheet of mica, reading as follows:

OPERATOR 5

THE WHITE HOUSE
Washington

To Whom It May Concern:

The identity of the bearer of this letter must be kept strictly confidential.

He is Operator 5 of the United States Intelligence Service.

The signature at the bottom of that letter was that of the President of the United States.

The little man's eyes popped as he read it, and he glanced up at Jimmy with awe.

"Geez!" he exclaimed. "I never seen a real Intelligence Agent before. I guess the lady was on the up-and-up, all right!"

Jimmy glared at him. "Come on! Talk up, will you? What did the lady tell you?"

The other straightened his coat where Jimmy's grip had disarranged it, and said:

"Well, mister, you see, it's like this. My name is Slips McGuire. The Slips part ain't my Christian name, but the boys all call me by it. My right given name, by which I was baptized—"

Jimmy fairly shouted at him: "Never mind that! What about the message?"

"Oh, yes, mister. I keep forgettin' that you're in a hurry. Well, you see, it was like this. I was over at the Hippodrome tonight, right after the explosion. I was just hangin' around, watchin' th' excitement, when I seen this here pretty young lady across the street, carryin' a handbag I followed her down the street—"

"Why did you follow her?" Jimmy demanded.

Slips McGuire hesitated, fidgeted from one foot to the other. "I—I was afraid you'd ask me that. But the young lady told me I could speak freely to you, as you was interested in bigger fish than pickpockets an' such like. Is that right?"

"Listen," Jimmy Christopher told him earnestly. "I don't care what you are. If you're a pickpocket, I don't care. I just want to get this message!" McGuire nodded. "That's what she said. An' she told me that you'd give me ten bucks if I brought this here message. Is that right?"

BESIDE HIMSELF with impatience, Jimmy took a ten-dollar bill from his pocket, handed it to the other. "Here you are. Now you better talk quick. Or else—"

"Okay, okay, mister. I'll spill everything. But I got to tell you the story from the beginning. You see, it was like this. I followed that there young lady because—" he hung his head shamefacedly—"because I figured she looked kind of excited, and excited dames is generally good pickin's. They don't notice what happens to their bags. Well, I follows this dame, and just as she gets down to the corner, I snips her purse from the handle around her arm. It was as easy as that. I ducks around the corner and takes a quick look in it, an' I see there's only three dollars and eighty-five cents in change and a press card showing that she's a reporter for the Amalgamated Press. Well, right away my conscience begins to bother me. She's only a poor member of the working class, like me. An' here I go deprivin' her of her last three-eighty-five. You know how it is when your conscience begins to bother you, don't you, mister?"

Jimmy groaned. "Yes, yes, I know all about it. Go on, man!"

127

McGuire shrugged. "I guess you do, seein' as how you're in the Secret Service. You fellows must run into a lot of interesting things like—Yes, yes, mister, I'll go on—" as Jimmy moved threateningly closer. "As I was sayin', my conscience started to annoy me, so I ducks back around the corner, figurin' to return the purse. An' I see this dame gettin' into a taxicab, and pointin' out a sedan a little ways up ahead. I just hear her say to the driver: 'Follow that car!' Well, I come runnin' after her, and I shouts: 'Hey, miss, you dropped your bag!' She turns around, an' it's the first time she notices she ain't got her purse. She starts to smile all over, and gee, I'll say she's pretty when she smiles. I got a daughter some place that's just about her age now. My wife Susie always used to say—all right, mister, I'll get back to the story." He shrank back from the clenched fist that Jimmy shook under his nose, gulped and went on.

"This here dame smiles at me an' says: 'Do you want to earn ten dollars?' I says: 'Sure, lady', an' she says: 'Get in the cab with me.' So I get in, an' we trail this here sedan. It goes over to a place on Riverside Drive, an' the lady says to me: 'Now you get out an' go as fast as you can to the Fleer Building, an' ask for Operator 5. Be sure you see Operator 5, an' no one else. Give him this note an' bring him here. Tell him I'll be waiting for him. Our man is inside.' So I hotfoots it over here—"

"Where's the note?" Jimmy demanded.

McGuire fished around in his pocket, pulled out a card, on which was written, in Diane's hand, the following hastily scrawled note:

Jimmy—I think this is the right trail. Come quickly, with this man, but trust no one else. Diane.

Jimmy Christopher glanced up from the note to find McGuire's eyes fixed on him in a birdlike gaze.

"Did you read this?" he asked.

McGuire shuffled. "No use my sayin' I didn't, mister."

"You know who it is the young lady is trailing?"

The little pickpocket nodded. "Yep. I got a look at him. It s Morty Kleed, that used to be Barney Broon's pay-off man."

"You know Kleed is a dangerous man?"

"I guess I do, mister."

"And yet you're willing to go back there? You may get killed."

"I'm willing."

"Why?"

McGUIRE LOWERED his eyes before Jimmy's piercing stare. His white, deft hands were twirling his battered hat "I'll tell you, mister. When I seen your lady friend was after Kleed, I'd of helped without gettin' paid at all." His thin features suddenly tightened, and his mouth twisted down at the corners. "Kleed an' Barney Broon done me a great hurt once—not me personal, but my daughter; the one I mentioned before. It was Barney Broon that tempted her to quit school, an' give her a job spottin' hold-up lays for his gang. That was seven years ago, when Broon an' Kleed weren't such big-timers. My little girl got picked up in a job out on the coast, an' she did three years in a reformatory in Frisco. When she come outta there, she kinda disappeared. I ain't never seen her since. Anything I can do against Broon or Kleed, mister, I'll do gladly!"

The sincerity in the little pickpocket's voice was unmistakable. Jimmy said: "All right, Slips. Wait here. I'll be back in a moment." He motioned to the agent who had come in with him. "Stay here with this man, L-4. And look out he doesn't take the electric light bulbs!"

L-4 grinned. "I'll be careful, Operator 5."

McGuire blinked, looked hurt. "Don't worry, mister. I won't take them bulbs. You couldn't sell no used bulbs to nobody!"

Jimmy smiled in spite of himself, hurried back to Z-7's office. He explained quickly what McGuire had told him, showed the note to Z-7 and the Secretary of War. The two of them had been busy on the phones. Z-7 had been getting last-minute reports from Intelligence offices in the riot areas, while the Secretary had been talking to Washington.

The Secretary said: "Young man, I've just talked to the President. He has agreed to authorize me to use the regular army in this emergency. Z-7 learns that mobs of highly armed men in trucks and stolen armored cars are marching on Washington from half a dozen cities. I should have taken your advice hours ago. The riots have spread all over the country. All those men are following their local leaders, who apparently are receiving orders from some central point. There will be dreadful bloodshed in every corner of the land before morning!"

Jimmy Christopher said quietly: "I'm sorry to hear that, sir." He could have added: "I told you so!" but he refrained. Instead he said: "The only way of avoiding a pitched battle between these mobs and the troops you are ordering out, is to locate the Scarlet

Baron's central headquarters. Perhaps this lead of Miss Elliot's will bring us closer to the Baron. I'll keep in touch with you."

The Secretary nodded. "It is more important to locate the Scarlet Baron now, than ever. He must be captured or killed, and these rioters must be made to know that their leader is no longer behind them. They are not isolated stragglers. They are almost an army in themselves—God knows how many thousands of them there are—and the few troops I could muster in a short time might not be able to stop them. This march on Washington may be just as successful in establishing a Fascist dictatorship here as similar *coups* have been in other countries in Europe. Tomorrow we may find ourselves governed by a bloody criminal!"

Jimmy nodded somberly. "I'll work as quickly as I can, sir. If Miss Elliot's lead proves to be a cold one, I'll return at once."

"Good luck to you, my boy," said the Secretary of War.

Jimmy Christopher left them, went out into the foyer. McGuire was pacing up and down, and L-4 was watching him closely.

"Well," Jimmy smiled, "did you keep him honest?"

L-4 grinned. "I can vouch for that, Operator 5. I didn't take my eyes off him for a minute. All he got out of here was a cigarette and a light that he mooched from me!"

"Okay," Jimmy said curtly to McGuire. "Let's go."

THEY STARTED out, but at the door McGuire stopped him. "Just a minute, mister." He jerked his head at L-4. "I guess your friend here was a little wrong." He fished in his coat pocket, brought out a nickeled automatic, which he offered, butt first, to L-4. "Ain't this your gun, mister?"

L-4's eyes widened, and his jaw fell open. He frantically pulled his coat open, glanced at the empty holster sagging under his armpit. "Well, I'll be damned!" he exclaimed. "How'd you get it?"

McGuire winked at Jimmy. "Easy," he said boastfully. "I got it while you was holdin' the lighter to my cigarette. There ain't a pocket in the world I can't pick!"

L-4 took the gun, red-faced, and returned it to his holster. "Boy," he said admiringly, "you're an artist!"

"And that ain't all," McGuire went on. "In case you want a smoke, here's your cigarettes back." He extended a package of smokes to the surprised Intelligence man.

L-4 dived into his own pocket, found it empty. "All right, guy," he said. "You can keep the butts. You earned them." Then he looked at Jimmy. "Better take that bird away from here before he gets my false teeth. And watch your pants while he's with you!"

Jimmy couldn't help laughing at L-4's discomfiture. McGuire beamed proudly. The little man took a pride in his unlawful skill, just as any other artist.

Jimmy Christopher led him out and down in the elevator. In the street he hailed a cab, instructed the driver, at McGuire's direction, to go across town and up along the Hudson River toward Seventy-Second Street.

On the way up, they passed patrols of National Guardsmen. Except for the uniformed soldiers, the streets were well-nigh deserted. There were faint streaks of dawn in the East, and the guardsmen seemed to be listless, dissatisfied with the task assigned them. Many of them sympathized with the Wealth-Sharing Movement. Jimmy could understand how a well-organized mob could expect little resistance from them. They would be unwilling to shoot down men who were seeking the necessities of life. Wealth-Sharing speakers and meetings had spread the insidious propaganda that no man need starve where there was so much surplus; and these guardsmen were of the very class to whom that appeal was directed.

Against Communists or other groups representing foreign influence, these National Guards would function effectively. But it was a little too much to expect them cold-bloodedly to shoot down their own countrymen—men fighting for a cause with which they themselves sympathized. Therein, Jimmy reflected, lay the damnable strength of the Scarlet Baron's organization. It was doubtful if even the regular army could be held in line against marching men seeking a so-called fair distribution of wealth. In Italy, in Germany, in many other countries, the record showed that the army had gone over to the Fascist side at the crucial moment.

Though Americans were a little harder to fool, the appeal of the Wealth-Sharing Movement was a powerful one. Backed as it was by a criminal of the top flight, it was far more dangerous even than any of the Fascist movements in Europe or South America.

THEIR CAB had been speeding up the elevated express highway. Now it swung off the highway, along the riverfront. Operator 5 glanced at McGuire. "Where's the place you left the young lady?"

"Right there!" McGuire pointed at a long, low shed, apparently a private yacht pier, jutting out into the river on the other side from the New York Central Railroad right-of-way.

Jimmy leaned forward, tapped on the glass. He said: "Pull up at the next corner."

They got out, and Jimmy scanned the street and the riverfront anxiously in search of Diane. She was nowhere in sight.

"That's funny," said McGuire. "I left her in the cab, right at this corner. Kleed went in that there shed."

Jimmy paid off the cab, and watched it depart. Then he scanned the long, low structure across the street. It was two stories, and in the row of windows along the upper floor there were lights. But the shades were drawn tightly.

McGuire whispered: "Maybe she went inside. Are you gonna raid the place or something?"

Jimmy shook his head. "I'm going to tell you something, McGuire. I think I can trust you." He had made up his mind to place his confidence in the little pickpocket. The man's sincerity had impressed him, in spite of his occupation. "Kleed is in some way tied up with the Scarlet Baron," he told the other. "The Scarlet Baron is behind the riots that are going on all over the country."

McGuire whistled softly. "Whew! An' who's the Scarlet Baron?"

"We don't know that—yet!" Jimmy said grimly. "We're trailing Kleed in the hope that he'll lead us to his chief. You understand how dangerous this work is. Are you still anxious to come along with me? If you are, I can use you tonight. But you don't have to if you're afraid."

"Afraid?" McGuire laughed nervously. "Sure I'm afraid. I ain't denyin' it. The Scarlet Baron has mopped up plenty of guys that went after him. But I ain't backin' out. I'll stick. Why? Because in the first place, there's Kleed. An' in the second place, I want to do my bit. I'm a pickpocket, see? A crook. But I'll fight anybody that's an enemy of the country. Why? Because it's a great country. Where else would a guy like me be able to make a living? In Europe, they'd put me in jail for life. Here, they let me out after six months, an' give me another chance. It's a great country, an' I'll help you fight for it!"

Jimmy could hardly keep from laughing. He had heard many reasons advanced for the patriotism that urged men into the nation's service. But it was the first time he had ever heard this particular reason.

He smiled. "All right, Slips. Maybe if we succeed, I can fix it so you don't have to be a pickpocket any more. You—" He stopped, drew McGuire into the shadow of the corner building before which they were standing. A taxicab was coming down the street, its headlights playing along the riverfront.

He pressed McGuire's arm, and they watched the cab stop near the corner, saw a man get out, pay the driver. The cab pulled away, and the passenger stood at the curb, drew a yellow telegraph from his pocket, read it as if he were checking its contents.

Jimmy said softly: "I'd like to know what's in that telegram!" He had a sudden hunch that it would be connected in some way with the building across the street.

McGuire grinned in the darkness, as he saw the man put the telegram back in his pocket. That's easy. Watch me!"

ABRUPTLY HE left Jimmy, stepped out from the shadow of the building, and Jimmy saw that he appeared to be staggering a little. He hiccoughed loudly, and the man at the curb turned, scowled, his hand going up to his armpit But he let it down again when he saw what appeared to be only a drunk weaving toward him.

McGuire had a cigarette between his fingers. He called out: "Hi-ya, pal? Got a light?"

The man shrugged, took a paper of matches from his pocket and handed it over. "G'wan, guy. Take a light an' scram!"

McGuire took the book of matches with a wavering hand, attempted to strike one, and failed ludicrously. He handed the book back "C'mon, pal, be a good guy, an' light it fer' me. I couldn't set fire to a barn, the way I feel right now!"

The man grinned, lit a match and held it for McGuire. The little pickpocket's hands moved so swiftly, so deftly, that Jimmy Christopher, from his place in the shadow, was compelled to silent admiration. With a speed that almost defied the eye, the yellow telegram was out of the man's pocket, and had disappeared. McGuire, puffing industriously at the cigarette, said:

"Thanks, pal. I'll do as much for you sometime," and started weaving an erratic course around the corner. Jimmy saw the man wait until he was gone, then walk across the street toward the long shed, and rap upon the door. It opened, and another man came out, who said something in a low voice. The visitor looked up and down the street to make sure he was not observed, then opened his coat, raised his left arm, and pulled away the shirt. The guard who had come out glanced at whatever was thus exposed, nodded, and stepped aside for the other to enter, then followed him in, closing the door.

In the moment that the door had been open, Jimmy had caught sight of a lighted interior, and his pulse raced at what he saw. For it was not a yacht that lay within that shed; it was a huge seaplane!

He moved along the building, keeping in the shadow, and turned the corner. McGuire was waiting for him, chuckling with glee. He handed over the telegram he had purloined from the man in the street.

"There you are, mister. I done that swell, didn't I?"

Jimmy smiled wryly. "It seems that crime *does* pay," he murmured. Where they stood they were sheltered from observation from the shed, and Jimmy took out his pencil flashlight, scanned the telegram. It was addressed to a parry named James Link, and read:

REPORT AT ONCE TO STATION NUMBER FOUR STOP COME READY FOR TRIP STOP WE ARE JOIN- ING BOSS STOP SHOW YOUR LETTER AT DOOR STOP BRING ANY OTHER BOYS YOU CAN FIND

MORT

Jimmy's mind was racing. The fact that Diane was not there, meant that she had either left without waiting for them, or had been caught by Kleed as she followed him. In the latter event, she would most probably be inside that shed. He gripped McGuire's shoulder.

"Slips," he said, "I'm going in there!"

McGuire stared at him. "Holy Mackerel, mister, you can't do that. The guy that went in there showed something to identify him. Some kind o' letter, like it says in the telegram."

"I know what he showed, Slips, and I'll have it, too. It's the letter 'B'—the work that the Scarlet Baron puts on his men!" He showed the electric branding instrument which he had in his pocket "Here's my passport into that place!"

McGuire's eyes were bright. "Could you give me a mark, too?"

Jimmy hesitated, then nodded. "All right. But first I've got to take this hypodermic needle out of this thing. We want the letter, but we don't want the dose that's in the needle."

He disregarded McGuire's questions, hurried him to the darkened doorway of one of the buildings along the side street, and extracted from his pocket a small leather case containing a number of skeleton keys. With these he worked on the door, got it open under McGuire's astounded eyes. He chuckled at the little pickpocket's amazement.

"You didn't know you were in the company of a housebreaker, did you? Come on in. We have to plug this branding machine into an electric socket to make it work. I'll tell you all about it inside!"

CHAPTER 10
AMERICA DOOMED!

LESS THAN twenty minutes later, two men slouched out of the darkened doorway of the side-street building. Though Slips McGuire retained his usual appearance, Jimmy

Christopher had undergone a subtle transformation. His nose was broader, his lips fuller, and his teeth, instead of showing brilliant white, appeared to be stained and blackened. It had taken only a small pair of nose plates, a little pigment, which he always carried with him, and half a dozen caps for his teeth. Jimmy had deemed it wise to alter his appearance to that extent, inasmuch as he was sure a general alarm would probably be out for Dave Orlando among the Scarlet Baron's henchmen.

The little touches of disguise, together with a change in his general bearing and method of walking, were sufficient to bury the personality of Dave Orlando. It had always been his theory that the art of effective disguise lay in small things; for the first glance is the one that gives the lasting impression. And at first glance, no one who had seen him in the character of Orlando would connect him with the dapper Chicago gunman.

Slips McGuire was a bit nervous, but he paced beside Jimmy with his jaw thrust out, and his chin up. The little pickpocket had himself undergone a different kind of transformation. For the first time in his life, perhaps, he was engaged in doing something that he did not need to be ashamed of. He was risking his life in an enterprise that was wormy of any man's sacrifice, and he was acting up to it.

They crossed the street, and Jimmy rapped at the door of the shed, as he had seen Link do. At once the door opened, and a squat man appeared, eyeing them suspiciously. Jimmy did the talking.

"We was told to report here," he said in clipped, sharp accents. He held his hand close to his necktie, where it was not far from the automatic in his shoulder holster, in case the guard should be suspicions. But the man at the door nodded, said: "Let's see your letters."

For answer, Jimmy and McGuire opened coats and shirt, raised their left arms to expose the still-raw letter "B" branded in their flesh. Fortunately—and Jimmy had counted on this— the light here was not very bright and the guard could not note that the brands were fresh and raw. He seemed satisfied, stood aside for them to enter.

"Come on in," he told them. "You're just in time. Five minutes more and we'd of been gone!"

A dozen men were in the shed. They had just finished rolling the huge seaplane down to the open end of the structure, and into the water. A pilot was climbing into the control room, and some of the others were mounting the short gangplank, while three of them held the ship close to the pier with rope.

Jimmy's blood raced as he saw Diane Elliot being led down a flight of stairs from the upper portion of the building, and conducted over the gangplank. Her hands were tied behind her, and she looked straight ahead of her, oblivious to the jests of the two men in whose charge she was.

Kleed was there, supervising the loading of the ship. He nodded to Jimmy and Slips, seeming to take them for granted, and said curtly:

"Get in, boys. We're taking off right away."

Jimmy nudged McGuire, and they mounted the gangplank right behind Diane. They were the last two in the passenger compartment, which had twelve seats, only nine of which were occupied, one by Diane. Jimmy seated himself directly behind her, watched while Kleed and another man passed up the aisle into the control room. Kleed was apparently the pilot.

The gangplank was removed, the hatch slid into place, and the plane was maneuvered out of the shed and into the river by two men in bathing suits and another in a row-boat. The two huge motors were turning over, and a moment later Kleed raised his hand in a signal, the men outside cast off the ropes, and the plane raced up the river, took off into the air.

THE MEN in the compartment all seemed to be tense, on edge. Jimmy glanced sideways at McGuire, who was sitting across the aisle. The little pickpocket apparently had never been up in a plane before, and his face was green. Several of the other men were also a bit sick. Jimmy gazed out of the window into the first streak of dawn in the East. His face set anxiously. While in the building on the side street where he had branded himself and Slips, he had made free with the phone in the office, and had called Z-7, told him what he planned to do. He had instructed the Intelligence Chief to call off all planes on patrol, so that the seaplane would have a free course toward its destination. These recruits for the forces of the Scarlet Baron must be allowed to reach their leader so that Jimmy could reach him also.

He had told Z-7 to have the patrol planes fly high, and if they spotted the ship, not to molest it, but to follow it discreetly. He was worried lest they hadn't been able to contact all the patrols. The last thing he wanted now was to have a couple of swift army pursuits swoop down upon them and force them to land.

He felt a bit easier as he noted that the sky was clear of planes.

If there were any in the air, they were flying high enough to avoid being seen by the pilot of the amphibian.

Jimmy Christopher's attention was drawn back to the compartment by the opening of the control-room door. He saw Kleed was coming into their compartment, having turned the controls over to his assistant.

Kleed stepped purposefully down the aisle, stopped alongside Diane Elliot, just in front of Jimmy. Diane was seated quite uncomfortably, due to the fact that her hands were tied behind her. She looked up at Kleed defiantly, but said nothing.

Kleed was a big man. His eyes were large, bulging a little, and seeming on the verge of popping out of his round, red face. He was inclined to be stout, and his hands were large, beefy. Jimmy wondered how such an ungainly-looking man was able to pilot a plane so skillfully; but he had done well, taking off smoothly, efficiently. There must be things in that big round head, Jimmy reflected, that did not show in the coarse, beefy face.

Kleed's mouth twisted in a grimace as he bent over Diane. "I hope you're comfortable, miss," he said in a high, piping voice, that came as rather a shock from that huge, ox-like man. "You're uninvited company, but I guess the boss won't mind me bringing you."

There was a trace in his voice of a culture that might one time have graced the man, but which had been smothered by association with the minions of the underworld.

Diane stared up at him defiantly, a cool smile on her white face. Jimmy, behind her, watching keenly from under drooping lids that gave an appearance of drowsiness, saw the open admiration in the glance which Kleed fixed upon Diane's softly modeled features, her trim shapely figure.

She spoke very low, her breasts heaving. "I—I made a mistake when I followed you. I should have known you'd be smart enough to spot me. I suppose I must—pay for that mistake."

Kleed grinned. "You bet, lady." He bent lower, said confidentially: "The only reason you're still alive is because the boss wired that he wants to talk to you. From the information I got out of your purse, he figures you're the girl that's been helping Operator 5. You're the girl that was with him when he threw that bomb in the Hippodrome. That was where you picked me up." He bent even closer, so that his bulging eyes were not a foot from Diane's face. *"Now who put you on my trail, miss?"*

DIANE FORCED a smile. "Don't you credit me with having been able to follow you without being told by anyone?"

Kleed returned her smile, grimly. "Don't dodge the question. Did Operator 5 come out of the Hippodrome alive?"

"I'm sorry," she said. "I can't tell you anything."

"You mean you won't!" His hairy, thick-fingered hand reached out, gripped her shoulder cruelly. "Listen, miss, the boss wired me to make you talk before we land. And you're going to talk, see? I want to know whether Operator 5 is still alive. And I want to know where he is now, if he's not dead. He must have told you where to get in touch with him. Will you speak up?"

Diane remained silent, though she winced under Kleed's grip on her shoulder. Jimmy Christopher could see that the big man's fingers were digging into her flesh painfully. She gasped, tried to twist away from him, but could not. Kleed's teeth were bared in a cruel smile. Jimmy saw that he was putting all his brute strength into that grip. Those powerful fingers were capable of almost dislocating her frail shoulder, and Operator 5 could barely restrain himself from leaping out of his seat.

His own shoulder throbbed fearfully, made him realize doubly the agony which Diane was undergoing. He glanced at the other men in the compartment Slips McGuire was looking at Kleed with hate-filled eyes, hands clenched in his lap. But he was waiting for his cue from Jimmy. The other men were watching amusedly, with a certain sadistic amusement betrayed on their faces. They were of the type who enjoy the sight of suffering in any form—when someone else is doing the suffering!

Suddenly Diane slumped in her seat, head dropping on her bosom. She had fainted from the pain. Kleed grunted in disgust, but did not release her. Instead, he lifted his left hand, brought it down in a resounding open-handed slap to the side of her head. The blow jerked Diane's head to one side, and she moaned, twitched spasmodically, and opened her eyes.

Kleed grinned, still holding on to her shoulder. "You don't faint on me, miss! I know a good treatment for fainting!" He slapped her again, and her right cheek burned a bright red.

And Jimmy Christopher gave way abruptly to the rage which was mounting inside of him. He came up out of his seat in a lightning lunge, bringing his left fist up in a blow that landed flush on the point of Kleed's chin with the thud of a sledgehammer pounding rock.

The fat man's head went up with a vicious jerk, and his ungainly body was smashed backward down the aisle, to crash into the door of the control room. The back of his head struck the door, and he collapsed into a quivering, unconscious mass of inertia. He lay there, still, with blood seeping from his nostrils, eyes turned up at an unnatural angle.

Diane gasped with sudden relief from the pressure of those cruel fingers on her flesh, and looked up with almost unbelieving wonder at the swiftly moving figure of Jimmy Christopher, whose artificially broad nose and altered features she failed to recognize.

Jimmy regretted his action almost in the moment that he struck. He was risking everything in order to save Diane some pain. He was still ignorant of the seaplane's destination, and by this unthinking attack upon Kleed he had perhaps discarded the last chance of learning it. But he had no time for regrets. The other men in the compartment leaped up.

Slips McGuire let out a howl of joy at sight of Kleed's supine figure and shouted at Jimmy: "Atta boy, mister!"

The ship rocked crazily as the man at the controls turned to stare back through the glass partition. The men in the compartment crowded into the aisle, shouting their hoarse rage at the man who had attacked their leader. A gun belched, reverberated with thunderous detonation, and a slug whined past Operator 5's head.

JIMMY CHRISTOPHER had struck Kleed with his left hand. Almost simultaneously, his right hand moved with lightning speed to his shoulder holster, came out with his automatic. Fiery lances of pain shot up his arm and shoulder, for this was the side that had been wounded in the fight with Paulson. But he gritted his teeth, leveled the gun and fired into the struggling mass of men seething in the aisle.

For perhaps two minutes, the compartment was filled with the smoke and thunder of belching guns. Their deafening roar drowned out the high drone of the twin motors, while the ship careened.

Jimmy Christopher kept on firing, regardless of the slugs that slapped past him, until he had emptied his automatic.

The nine shots that he pumped from the automatic disposed of six of his assailants. Their bodies slid along the aisle in gruesome fashion. Three men were left on their feet, with guns in hand. Jimmy Christopher's automatic was empty, and the three wolfishly bent forward, guns beaded on his stomach. They were not going to ask questions. In a moment they were going to send a hail of lead into him. They had seen what he had done to Kleed, they had seen their fellows drop before his flaming gun. Death stared Jimmy Christopher in the face. He raised his gun to throw it at the nearest. His last gesture was to be a fighting one.

And suddenly, help came from an unexpected source. Above the top of the seat directly beside him, there appeared a bald head and a wizened face, followed by a long-fingered hand clutching a pearl-handled revolver. Again and again the little gun exploded—six times, with a cracking, barking sound at each fall of the hammer. Magically, the aisle was cleared of living men. McGuire popped out from behind the shelter of his seat, and waved the revolver wildly.

"Yea, boy!" he almost screamed. "We gave it to 'em!"

Diane was staring up at Jimmy Christopher with dawning

recognition. "Jimmy!" she gasped, with astonishment reflected in her glad warm smile. "Jimmy! You—you wonder!"

But Operator 5 did not hear her. He had launched himself over the bodies littering the aisle, toward the door of the control room. Through the glass partition he had seen the pilot reaching over to the wireless key on the panel at the left of the instrument board. The man was going to send out a warning.

Jimmy reached the door, wrenched it open just as the pilot swung away from the key and snatched up a gun from a clip screwed into the instrument panel. Jimmy gave him no time to raise it. His left fist, bunched into a hard ball, caught the man behind the ear.

THE SHIP was jerking violently. It had fallen into a side-spin, and for five minutes Jimmy Christopher fought the controls with the consummate skill of a desperate, seasoned flyer. At the end of that time, he had the plane out of the spin, and he turned grimly to see Slips McGuire and Diane standing just behind them. Slips had freed her hands while Jimmy was righting the ship.

Jimmy smiled at him. He was beginning to like the little pickpocket. It had taken pluck to stand up to those three gunmen with his little revolver.

"You're all right, Slips," Jimmy told him. "I guess you saved the day." He glanced up at Diane. "Di, I'm afraid—"

He was interrupted by the buzzer of the wireless phone cradled near his left hand. He frowned. Apparently the pilot had managed to send out some sort of call signal over the wire-

Jimmy Christopher kept on firing!

less, and, failing to receive a following message, the party at the other end was calling on the phone.

He got up from the pilot's seat, said to Diane: "Take it over, Di. Keep her course due south; that seems to be the direction Kleed was taking."

Diane nodded eagerly, seated herself and took the controls. Her cheek was still streaked with red where Kleed had struck her, and she was breathing hard from the excitement of the last few moments; but her hands were firm and capable on the controls, her eyes cool as they flicked over the dials on the instrument board.

The buzzer was still sounding, and Jimmy Christopher said: "Yes?"

Immediately, a faint voice barked: "Kleed! That you?"

Jimmy said: "Right!"

"Did you signal? I got your code, but couldn't raise you. Anything wrong?"

"Nothing is wrong," Jimmy said, changing his voice slightly to conform to the tone he had heard Kleed use. He had little fear of the subterfuge being detected, for the other's voice was not coming over any too clearly either. "I just wanted to ask what I should do with the girl. She won't talk."

A chuckle sounded at the other end. "She's a hard one, eh? I've got that kid here with me, and he won't talk either. I expect to hit Leander in three hours—"Jimmy gave an involuntary start, for here, unexpectedly, was thrust into his lap the information he despaired of getting—"and we'll jockey the kid against the girl. But it won't make much difference whether they talk or not, once we reach Leander. The riots have gone over in every city except New York. It's lucky that Operator 5 can't be everywhere at once. I'm concentrating in the South. The rioters are marching on Washington from three directions at once. The government is afraid to use the regular army, and we're sitting pretty. Tomorrow I'll declare myself dictator of America. And the fun begins. See you soon, Kleed."

The line went dead, and Jimmy slammed the instrument down, reached frantically for the telegraph key on the other side of Diane. With hasty fingers he clicked out the code signal for Intelligence headquarters, clicked it again and again, then waited until he got the answering signal. Then he feverishly rapped out the following coded message:

Z-7... SCARLET BARON STILL IN SEAPLANE SOMEWHERE ON THE WAY TO LEANDER PRISON ON FLORIDA COAST... ORIGINAL THEORY SUBSTANTIATED... HAVE NO DOUBT NOW THAT BARON IS REALLY BARNEY BROON... THROW EVERY AVAILABLE PLANE AROUND LEANDER TO KEEP BROON FROM ENTERING... WILL KEEP IN TOUCH WITH YOU.

HE WAITED a moment while Diane guided the plane southward in the rapidly brightening day. Behind him, in the passenger compartment, Slips McGuire was stepping among the bodies of the men in the aisle, collecting weapons. Soon an answering message came over the instrument from Z-7:

IMPOSSIBLE TO STOP BROON FROM REACH-
ING LEANDER... ALL AVAILABLE PLANES ARE
MILES BEHIND HIM IN CORDON WE THREW
AROUND CHESAPEAKE BAY... SECRETARY OF WAR
IS ORDERING TROOPS TO MOVE ON LEANDER...
WILL HOLD OFF ATTACK UNTIL CERTAIN BROON
IS WITHIN... WE HAVE TRIED TO COMMUNICATE
WITH LEANDER BUT CAN GET NO ANSWER...
WARDEN THERE IS PROBABLY IN LEAGUE WITH
BROON....

Suddenly the key became silent. Jimmy glanced at Diane,
who was gazing tensely ahead. He swung away from it, only to
turn quickly back as the instrument sprang into life once more.
Another message was coming in from Z-7. And Jimmy's lips
tightened as he got its meaning:

HAVE JUST RECEIVED MESSAGE FROM GOVERN-
MENT PROVING GROUNDS AT ABERDEEN MARY-
LAND... MOB OF RIOTERS DETOURED FROM
MARCH ON WASHINGTON AND SWARMED OVER
GOVERNMENT ORDNANCE PROVING GROUNDS
AT ABERDEEN... TWO COMPANIES OF INFAN-
TRY MASSACRED... TEN FOURTEEN-INCH GUNS
MOUNTED ON RAILROAD ARE NOW IN HANDS OF
RIOTERS... ALSO FIFTEEN ANTIAIRCRAFT GUNS...
THEY CAN BLAST WASHINGTON OFF MAP... ONLY
HOPE TO LOCATE SCARLET BARON... FOR GOD'S
SAKE DO NOT FAIL....

CHAPTER 11
THE BATTLE OF
LEANDER PRISON

L EANDER PRISON, brooding on a triangular peninsula off the Florida coast, possessed the doubtful honor of
housing some of the most notorious criminals whom Federal
agents had brought to justice in the last few years.

At one time, the gloomy pile had been a fortress of the proud
Spanish Dons. Taken over with the rest of Florida by the United
States, its coral walls had been buttressed with rock, its moat
filled in, and heavy guns placed upon the escarpments. It became
an army post; then, with the development of the huge coast-
guard guns now in use, it had become once more neglected,
the walls allowed to crumble; its pristine glory vanished. Few
people visited it, for the road by which it could be reached was
a narrow one, winding through tracts of Everglade land that
offered death to the unwary.

At last, however, the government decided that its very inac-
cessibility to land made it desirable for the purpose of housing
those major criminals whom it particularly wanted to keep from
escape. Leander was made a penitentiary....

The swift darkness of the semi-tropics had already descended
upon the old building. Somehow, a stranger wandering by
chance on to that peninsula, would have sensed that there was
something weird, unholy in the atmosphere. The one road by
which the prison could be reached from the mainland was
heavily barricaded with huge piles of coral rock. Behind those

barricades men crouched in hastily thrown-up machine-gun emplacements. They were not United States soldiers.

On the other side of the building, which abutted on the water, three huge seaplanes were being drawn up on to the landing pier on rollers, pulled by small tractors.

Inside, in the room marked: "Warden's Office," there were five people.

One of these was Warden Jerome Manly, the man who had told the Secretary of War that Barney Broon was safe in his cell for the night. Warden Manly's face was pale, ashen, as he sat in a corner.

Behind the warden's desk sat the Scarlet Baron—Barney Broon. Facing him, standing, were Cele Volney and the man, Franz, who had flown with the Baron in the second seaplane. And leaning with his back to the wall, blood seeping from his forehead, hands tied, was Tim Donovan.

The Scarlet Baron was smiling, nodding in satisfaction. "You did very well, Manly," he was saying. "Telling the Secretary of War that I was in my cell was just the right thing."

He winked at Franz, who was looking at him with admiration. "They've seized the proving grounds at Aberdeen, and they've raided the coast guard stations up and down the coast."

Franz took a step forward. "But the sea, boss. They can send ships—"

Broon laughed shortly. "We've got long-range guns on the walls. We can stand off any ships for twenty-four hours. And by that time there'll be a new government in Washington. The fleet will take orders from—me!" He glanced across the room, frowned at Tim Donovan, who was glaring at him. "You, boy! Whom were you sending that message to when you were caught at the radio in the plane?"

Tim Donovan straightened his shoulders with an effort, raised his bound hands and wiped blood from his eyes with his sleeve. The lad attempted a feeble grin. "I was sending a message to Santa Claus," he said. "I want a pop-gun next Christmas."

Broon did not grow angry. Instead, he smiled thinly. "If it were important," he said, "I'd *make* you talk. As it is, I'll just put you in the cell where I'm supposed to be. Kleed is bringing a girl here, and he's probably found out everything we need to know about your friend, Operator 5."

The boy started, his eyes widening. "You mean—you've got Diane Elliot?"

Broon grinned. "She'll be here in the plane in a few minutes. You'll—"

HE STOPPED as a knock sounded at the door, and one of his men entered, flushed with triumph. "We just got the flash, boss! The rioters have hit Washington. There weren't enough federal troops to stop 'em. They're storming the White House now, and demanding that the President resign. They started fires in the federal buildings on the way to the White House, and the city is burning. The men we had planted in the Anacostia Naval Station acted on schedule. They killed the commanding officer, and took over. We got complete control!"

Broon beamed. "Excellent. Send out this proclamation." He took from the desk a sheet of paper. Before handing it over, he glanced through it, his eyes glowing with unholy ego. It read:

To the People of the United States:

The government having abdicated, we, the Wealth-Sharers, have taken over. All shall have equal wealth. From this time on, there shall be no poverty. There is enough in this land for all of us. Our Leader will divide everything equally with the common people.

Do not resist the new government. To do so will mean quick death. To join us will mean wealth for each of you.

By this proclamation the center of government is hereby moved from Washington to Leander. The first Commander of the Nation is hereby proclaimed the unconditional ruler of the United States. You have been waiting eagerly to learn who he is. His name is The Scarlet Baron! The man who has always taken from the rich to give to the poor, is now at the head of your destinies. Follow him loyally and you will be happy. Defy him—and you will die!

The name of the Scarlet Baron was signed to the strange document. Broon handed it to his man, ordered: "Send that out over the wires. Order it published in every newspaper in every city."

The man took the proclamation, hastened from the room. Broon smiled across his desk at Cele Volney. "Well, Cele, here we are. You never expected that I'd be boss of the whole damn country, did you?"

She lowered her eyes. "It's—it's swell!"

Broon motioned to Franz: "Take the kid down and put him in a cell. Then—"

Another knock came, and a second messenger entered. Broon frowned. "Well?"

"There's some federal troops marching against us on Highway 1, boss. They're from Fort Lauderdale and Fort Pierce. A couple of scouts just came in. They report there's about fifteen hundred of 'em."

"All right. We'll take care of them!"

Franz had stepped over to Tim Donovan, seized him by the arm. "Come on, boy. I got to put you away the boss says."

Tim had been watching Broon, had heard him give the order to turn the big gun on the advancing federal troops. Now his eyes darted about the room for some means of escape, some way to ward off the disaster. But there was nothing. He allowed himself to be led from the room.

The boy felt hopeless, low in spirits. There was no sign that Jimmy Christopher was still alive, no chance of frustrating the mad plan of the new dictator.

The corridor led along the outside of the wall, with apertures through which the jetty below could be seen. The three seaplanes in which Broon and his men had arrived were all up on land now, and Franz, as he led the boy along, glanced out and exclaimed, half to himself: "There's Kleed!" He stopped, still holding on to Tim, his eyes on another trim plane that was just gliding in. TIM'S HEART went cold. He knew what Broon had said, that Diane would be on that plane. His lips tightened, and there was a suspicious moisture in his eyes. Here, it seemed, was the end of the trail for all three of them —Jimmy Christopher, Diane, and himself. That Operator 5 was dead, he could not doubt; else he would have been heard from in some fashion.

Listlessly, Tim watched the seaplane being edged over to the pier, watched the hatch open and a man emerge. Suddenly, Tim's figure tautened, his eyes narrowed.

The man who had just poked his head out of the hatch was carrying a submachine gun under his arm. He was followed by a girl whom Tim recognized as Diane, and by another, smaller man. They all had sub-machine guns. But the thing that caught and held the boy's attention was the form of the first man.

That figure was familiar!

Tim Donovan could have sworn that man was Operator 5!

The things that happened next made him certain that he was right. The men who had assisted in tying up the seaplane must have expected something, for Tim saw him seize Jimmy Christopher's arm, peer into his face. And Jimmy Christopher sent a smashing blow into that man's face, sending him reeling backward.

Then, under Tim Donovan's still startled gaze, Jimmy Christopher, with Diane and the thin man behind her, started to run toward the entrance of the building, directly below Tim.

Franz exclaimed: "My God! That's not Kleed!" His hand went into his coat, came out with an automatic. He bent out over the embrasure, aimed at Jimmy's running figure below.

But Tim Donovan, acting with swift desperation, lifted up his bound hands, clenched his fists, and brought them down in a thudding blow to Franz's head.

Tim Donovan shouted: "Jimmy! Jimmy! Come and get 'em!"

But his voice was drowned by the rattle of machine-gun fire from the yard below. He glanced over Franz's unconscious body, saw that the weapons of Jimmy and his two companions were barking in swift staccato tune as the three of them ran into the entrance of the building.

Tim turned and ran for the stairway. Men were scurrying about in alarm, not knowing what had happened. The door of Broon's room opened, and the Scarlet Baron came rushing out with Cele Volney behind him. Broon saw the limp figure of Franz across the embrasure; saw Tim at the head of the stairs, and his face assumed a terrible expression. He had a gun in his hand, and he leveled it at Tim.

The boy launched himself down the stairs. With his hands bound in front of him, he couldn't keep his balance, and went toppling down the flight. At the foot of the stairs, a half dozen of Broon's men were gathered, backing away from the grim semi-circle made by Jimmy, Diane, and Slips McGuire at the door.

The men at the foot of the stairs were bunched close, and two of them had submachine guns. Jimmy had ceased firing, and was advancing grimly, when Tim Donovan's hurtling body went crashing into the group of men facing him. They were thrown into confusion, and Jimmy exclaimed: "Tim!"

He threw himself forward, upon the men who had turned to pummel Tim. His heavy machine gun swung through the air like a club as he beat it down upon the heads of the men. Slips McGuire rushed in too, flailing about him with his Tommy-gun, using it as a club also.

159

From the top of the stairs there came the repeated crack of a revolver, and Jimmy Christopher looked up to see Broon at the top, firing down into the mess of struggling men. The Scarlet Baron didn't seem to mind if he hit his own men, as long as he got Operator 5!

JIMMY CHRISTOPHER raised his Tommy-gun, and Broon ducked away from the head of the stairs, raced out of sight. For a moment there showed, behind him, the white face of Cele Volney; and Slips McGuire, beside Jimmy, uttered a startled, heart-wrung exclamation.

"Cele!" he shouted: "My daughter!"

Jimmy had only time to spare him a glance. Diane was standing grimly near them, holding at bay the men who had jumped on Tim. Three of them were lying still on the floor, their heads cracked open by the improvised clubs of Operator 5 and Slips McGuire. The other three stood with their hands in the air.

Tim Donovan scrambled to his feet, feeling himself gingerly. "Oh boy!" he shouted. "That was some scrap!" Suddenly his face darkened. "Jimmy!" We got to get upstairs. Troops are marching from Fort Pierce and Lauderdale!"

"I know," Jimmy told him. "We communicated with them by radio. We've got to signal them when it's okay to storm the place." He strode into a corner, seized a lantern that was burning there for semaphore signaling, and handed it to Diane. "Flash them, Di—"

"No, no!" Tim Donovan exclaimed, seizing his arm. "Not yet, Jimmy. There's a big gun on the walls. Broon is turning it on them… he'll wipe the troops—!"

160

While they had been talking, a close-packed crowd of men had appeared from the rear of the building, where the barracks rooms were located. These had guns and rifles, and they raised a shout at seeing Jimmy and the others.

Operator 5, his face grim and bleak, raised the machine gun, sent a spray of lead screaming into their midst. The group dissolved. Many lay dead on the floor, while others ran away screaming.

"Let's go!" Jimmy shouted, and started up the stairs. Diane followed him, with Tim close behind. McGuire swung his Tommy toward the three whom Diane had been covering, rapped out: "Scram!"

The three backed away hastily, tripping over the dead bodies of their comrades in their haste to get away from the muzzle of the weapon. When they had disappeared, McGuire followed Jimmy.

Jimmy Christopher had already reached the turret where the huge gun was being loaded. These men of the Scarlet Baron's must have numbered among them some skillful gunners—probably ex-soldiers or men planted among the troops for propaganda purposes. They were working with grim efficiency, and a shell was already being placed in the breech. The Scarlet Baron had retreated to the concrete slab upon which the gun rested, and half a dozen of his plug-uglies were guarding the terrace around it.

Jimmy dropped flat to the ground, with the sub-machined gun raised in front of him. He let off a burst, and the men firing at him were mowed down as with a huge scythe. But the Baron had moved behind the huge steel gun, and was safe. From his place of vantage he sent an occasional shot in Jimmy's direction.

Diane and Tim crouched just around the corner of the wall, behind Operator 5. They would have pushed forward, but Jimmy blocked their way.

Suddenly Operator 5's gun ceased to chatter. He had exhausted the drum! He dropped the weapon, reached around to grasp the one that Diane was offering him. But the Baron sensed that this was his opportunity. He shouted hoarsely:

"Get him, boys! His drum's empty!"

JIMMY SNATCHED Diane's Thompson, turned it on the charging men. He shouted; "Give the signal, Di. I'll keep them away from the gun!" He hardly waited to finish, but let off another burst. The charge stopped, the men scampered for cover.

Behind him, Jimmy heard Diane moving, saw out of the corner of his eye that she was waving the lantern at one of the embrasures. The Scarlet Baron shouted in rage, poked his head and arm out from behind the big gun, and aimed at Diane. Jimmy pressed his finger down on the trip of the machine gun, and the Baron's head disappeared in a rain of lead that practically tore it from his shoulders. His bloody body slumped to the concrete slab. The Scarlet Baron was dead! The men on the terrace stood stunned in silence at the sight of their dead leader....

Jimmy Christopher shouted to them: "Drop your weapons and surrender. The Federal troops will be here in a few minutes. You have no chance!"

Dully, the men let their guns fall to the ground, lifted their hands. Out from behind Jimmy there rushed the thin form of Slips McGuire. He paid no attention to the prisoner, but made a bee line for a still, small body on the ground not far from the wall, and knelt beside it.

"Cele!" he said in a hushed voice. He looked up at Jimmy, and there was unutterable pain in his eyes. "She was hit by a stray bullet. She's dead!" He gulped. "She was my daughter. The girl I told you about!"

Jimmy came up beside him, put a hand on his shoulder. There was nothing to say. He turned away, left McGuire alone.

In the distance, a bugle sounded in answer to Diane's signal. She kept on waving the lantern. Tim Donovan came up beside Jimmy. "What do we do now?" the boy asked.

Operator 5 looked down at him affectionately. "Do? Haven't you done enough? We're through, Tim, through! When the troops come, we're all through!" He bent and untied Tim's wrists. "Go stretch them, kid. I'm going to send out an announcement that the Scarlet Baron is dead. When that's flashed over the country, the revolution will die!"

Tim rubbed his hands, stuck his tongue out at the men standing with their hands in the air. Then his glance fell on a small structure jutting out from the building onto the terrace. "Jimmy!" he said. "There's a radio room. Want me to send out the flash?"

"Okay, Tim. See if you can pick up Z-7. Get him to give out the announcement. There'll be a lot of bloodshed tonight before the news percolates to all the rioters, but things ought to be under control by morning."

Tim left him, heading for the radio room, and Jimmy turned

to Slips McGuire, looked somberly at the little pickpocket, who had arisen from beside the body of his daughter.

Diane had put down her lantern, come up to them. The prisoners, cowed, were standing close to the wall, watching them.

Tim Donovan came out of the radio room. His eyes were shining. "Jimmy! I got Z-7, and he put on the Secretary of War. When I told them the news the Secretary almost went nuts. He wants to get you a Congressional Medal!"

Jimmy shrugged.

"But that isn't all, Jimmy," the boy went on swiftly. "Z-7 had a pretty funny message for you. He said for you to quit loafing, and to get back to Washington just as fast as you can make it!"

"What?"

Tim grinned. "He says that while you've been vacationing with this Scarlet Baron business, hell has been popping in the international situation. The war-dogs of Europe and the Orient have just cooked up a scheme for invading the United States. Z-7 says you'll have to exert every bit of your skill to break the syndicate. Espionage and sabotage are more prevalent now than ever before. After this, the G-Men will have to do their own worrying. Let's all get back into that seaplane!"

Operator 5 smiled slowly at the boy's enthusiasm. No one knew better than he the perils menacing our land in the turbulent days to come.

He saw Slips McGuire looking at him queerly. "You're a lucky guy, mister," McGuire said. "You got this dame, and this kid an' you'll go on being a big shot in the Intelligence. Me, I got nothin' and nobody!" He gulped, glanced down at Cele Volney's body.

FROM BELOW there came the sounds of marching feet, crisp commands. The first of the troops had arrived, were encountering no opposition below. Those men who had been downstairs had fled. The way was open to the federal soldiers.

Jimmy put an arm around the narrow shoulders of the little pickpocket. "I'm going to take you away from your old life, Slips. I'm going to give you a job. I'll make you forget about all—this!"

McGuire's thin face turned up to him. "You—mean that, mister?"

"I do. You and Di and Tim and I—we'll work together from now on. And from what I know of all of you, the country will be plenty safe!"

"B-but—" faltered Slips, "they won't take me in the Intelligence—"

"They'll take you," Jimmy Christopher said grimly, "if I have to start a revolution of my own to do it!"

THE SPIDER

- ❏ #1: The Spider Strikes — $13.95
- ❏ #2: The Wheel of Death — $13.95
- ❏ #3: Wings of the Black Death — $13.95
- ❏ #4: City of Flaming Shadows — $13.95
- ❏ #5: Empire of Doom! — $13.95
- ❏ #6: Citadel of Hell — $13.95
- ❏ #7: The Serpent of Destruction — $13.95
- ❏ #8: The Mad Horde — $13.95
- ❏ #9: Satan's Death Blast — $13.95
- ❏ #10: The Corpse Cargo — $13.95
- ❏ #11: Prince of the Red Looters — $13.95
- ❏ #12: Reign of the Silver Terror — $13.95
- ❏ #13: Builders of the Dark Empire — $13.95
- ❏ #14: Death's Crimson Juggernaut — $13.95
- ❏ #15: The Red Death Rain — $13.95
- ❏ #16: The City Destroyer — $13.95
- ❏ #17: The Pain Master — $13.95
- ❏ #18: The Flame Master — $13.95
- ❏ #19: Slaves of the Crime Master — $13.95
- ❏ #20: Reign of the Death Fiddler — $13.95
- ❏ #21: Hordes of the Red Butcher — $13.95
- ❏ #22: Dragon Lord of the Underworld — $13.95
- ❏ #23: Master of the Death-Madness — $13.95
- ❏ #24: King of the Red Killers — $13.95
- ❏ #25: Overlord of the Damned — $13.95
- ❏ #26: Death Reign of the Vampire King — $13.95
- ❏ #27: Emperor of the Yellow Death — $13.95
- ❏ #28: The Mayor of Hell — $13.95
- ❏ #29: Slaves of the Murder Syndicate — $13.95
- ❏ #30: Green Globes of Death — $13.95
- ❏ #31: The Cholera King — $13.95
- ❏ #32: Slaves of the Dragon — $13.95
- ❏ #33: Legions of Madness — $12.95
- ❏ #34: Laboratory of the Damned — $12.95
- ❏ #35: Satan's Sightless Legion — $12.95
- ❏ #36: The Coming of the Terror — $12.95
- ❏ #37: The Devil's Death-Dwarfs — $12.95
- ❏ #38: City of Dreadful Night — $12.95
- ❏ #39: Reign of the Snake Men — $12.95
- ❏ #40: Dictator of the Damned — $12.95
- ❏ #41: The Mill-Town Massacres — $12.95
- ❏ #42: Satan's Workshop — $12.95
- ❏ #43: Scourge of the Yellow Fangs — $12.95
- ❏ #44: The Devil's Pawnbroker — $12.95
- ❏ **NEW:** #45: Voyage of the Coffin Ship — $12.95

THE WESTERN RAIDER

- ❏ #1: Guns of the Damned — $13.95
- ❏ #2: The Hawk Rides Back from Death — $13.95
- ❏ #3: Gun-Call for the Lost Legion — $13.95
- ❏ #4: The Law of Silver Trent — $13.95

G-8 AND HIS BATTLE ACES

- ❏ #1: The Bat Staffel — $13.95

CAPTAIN SATAN

- ❏ #1: The Mask of the Damned — $13.95
- ❏ #2: Parole for the Dead — $13.95
- ❏ #3: The Dead Man Express — $13.95
- ❏ #4: A Ghost Rides the Dawn — $13.95
- ❏ #5: The Ambassador From Hell — $13.95

DR. YEN SIN

- ❏ #1: Mystery of the Dragon's Shadow — $12.95
- ❏ #2: Mystery of the Golden Skull — $12.95
- ❏ #3: Mystery of the Singing Mummies — $12.95

CAPTAIN ZERO

- ❏ #1: City of Deadly Sleep — $13.95
- ❏ #2: The Mark of Zero! — $13.95
- ❏ #3: The Golden Murder Syndicate — $13.95